Chasin' It

By E. Scrill

STREET INK PUBLICATIONS®

Street Ink

www.streetinkbooks.com

ISBN: 978-0-9816399-9-4

First Edition

Manufactured in the United States of America.

PROLOGUE

Raynard sat across from his homeboy Ike at Coney Island on McNichols and Schaefer. He knew his services were needed when he was first asked by Ike to meet him there. The two were always tight, but Ike had made smarter moves in life than Raynard, and seemed to be living a way much better life. He had the nice cars, clothes and women. Raynard wasn't doing *all* bad, he still had his woman, and knew how to hustle between SSI checks.

Ike and Raynard came up together, but after Ike went away to school and Raynard started experimenting with harder pieces of the streets, the two kind of grew apart. Ike might scoop Raynard up for a night out here and there, but Raynard was never invited around if Ike had a function at his home in the hills or just had a couple of chicks and needed a wing man.

"Man," Ike began. "You been with ol' girl a long time. I remember that time I came home from school, and you was workin' for her cousin over at that buildin'."

"Oh, yeah. That was her big cousin, Johnny. Yup, Johnny Cash. They put me on the team when they was gettin' all that money sellin' mixed jive! He had a helluva recipe, boy, I tell ya. The fiends loved him."

"You say it was his recipe, huh?" Ike asked with raised eyebrows.

"Hell yeah. That's what it was. They called it jive, but they kept comin'! He just had a better recipe than them other niggas. I mean, shit, they was all sellin' heroin."

Raynard watched as Ike rubbed his chin. Ike was all in. Raynard knew Ike loved when he dropped that good, grimy ghetto stuff. Raynard loved droppin' it on him. Fools never really seem to act a fool unless they have an audience of some sort. Ike was always Raynard's audience, and Raynard kept him entertained.

"I found some pictures of you and your girl from back in the day," Ike said.

Raynard sniffed. "Fuck that fat bitch!" Raynard let Ike chuckle a bit before continuing with, "Yeah, see even today, if you got the right recipe, yo dope gonna sell like three-dollar whores!"

"So, was that the mixed jive they was smokin' in that big ass pipe?" Ike asked.

"Oh, yea that hookah? Naw, that was 'cain. Them old heads used to put Cognac in the bottom, then drop that 'cain in the top part and get fucked up."

"Damn!" Ike said.

Raynard took the square napkin from underneath his water glass and folded it diagonally, so that it formed a triangle. He crumpled a pointy end deep into his left nostril and twisted it a couple revolutions before taking it out to look at it. As he peered at the crimson tip, he noticed Ike in his peripheral vision making a "yuck" face. In an attempt to get Ike's mind off of being so grossed out, Raynard continued with, "Yup. But, you know all the dope they smoked with that cognac in the bottom turned into a lot of residue. They called it doo-doo balls. Shit, I remember one time them niggas ran outta 'cain and smoked the doo-doo balls!"

"Damn!" Ike said, before joining Raynard in laughter. "Well, playa, what's up with you?"

"What? You mean with the powder?"

Ike nodded.

"I still fuck around a li'l," Raynard said, speaking boldly, but moving his eyes to the floor. "Matter of fact, I could use a li'l one-on-one right about now."

"One-on-one?"

Pointing to one nostril Raynard said, "One…" He moved his finger to the other nostril and said, "…On one."

"My boy, Lenard got a good recipe."

"Oh, yeah?" Raynard asked in disbelief. He never heard of Ike having any other real connects to the street, let alone the bag. Not at all worried about Ike being on anything shady; he just wanted a blast. "Let me check 'em out."

"Ok, but the thing is…it's like a tester…"

"A freebie?" Raynard asked in a voice like Yoda, trying to make Ike laugh at the same time letting out his joy of a free blast.

"It's some kinda new synthetic shit they came up with."

Cutting Ike off, Raynard said, "Oh, yea, I had synthetic 'cain before. Man, 'cain is 'cain!" He sniffed a few times.

"Yeah, he just strap you in first…"

"What? Strap me in? What type of Frankenstein shit? You gon' be in the room, right?" Raynard asked, knowing it was not normal to be strapped down to test dope, but still couldn't pass on the free blow. "So, they just wanna get their recipe right, and they need me to test the product?"

"Right!" Ike said.

Raynard followed Ike to the old Summit Medical Center building a few blocks west of Greenfield. He noted the illegal power hook up out back, and knew it was Moose's handiwork.

Inside the building, Raynard looked around, already figuring he was on the janky end of things from the gate.

A tall, dark figure entered the room they were in.

"Raynard, you know Lenard, right?"

"Oh, yeah! Wassup, baby? Y'all rich niggas don't even fuck witcha mans in the hood like you s'posed to."

Lenard smiled, apparently happy to see Raynard as well. "I'm the one who suggested calling you, buddy!"

"Oh, it was you?" Raynard looked at Ike with a raised eyebrow. "And all the time I thought my main man Ike was pluggin' me with a hook up!" He turned and looked at Ike who was over at the sink sounding as if he were washing silverware. Raynard was stabbed by the stressful fact that he may not even be at the top of Ike's list if a free blow came about. He shook off the thought and continued with, "Well, shit, do you still have the hook up on the scripts?"

Lenard thought for a moment. "Scripts?" He politely held out his left hand, directing Raynard to a reclining chair that sat in the middle of the floor, complete with stirrups. The chair was modified to include a strap that would fit around ones arms and one lower to harness the legs.

"You know, the prescriptions you had the hook up on. Them bars and footballs and stuff."

"Oh, you mean the medication?"

"Yeah. Can you still get that shit?" Raynard fast-talked while being strapped in. "Niggas I know be lookin' for lean and Roxies…"

Obviously sensing Raynard's chatter to be a sign of nervousness, Lenard placed a hand on Raynard's shoulder. "Relax. Be honest with me…when was the last time you did cocaine?"

"Yesterday. Shit, y'all was right on time with this, too…"

Lenard cut him off by placing the hand on his shoulder again. "You can never mention this to anyone. What we are going to give you is unlike any of the coke currently being sold on the streets."

Raynard's grin flexed with a mind of its own. "Yay-yay! The uncut plug! I'm ready!"

The last thing Raynard remembered was seeing a skinny, metal object approaching his face. It forked and had two small spoon ends at the tip. Each spoon end had a micro mound of white powder on it. He didn't remember inhaling, but did remember seeing Ike in his peripheral vision, hawk-eyeing the whole situation.

CHAPTER 1

Raynard could see fear in his friend Ike's face as the two crept through the alley toward Pat's backyard. "Yeah, this bitch think she slick!" he whispered to Ike. "Like we gon just let her get away with not payin' us for all the work we done cleanin' out her funky ass basement!"

"I'm hip," said Ike, seemingly charged by Raynard's words. He took the lead as they passed through the gate leading to Pat's backyard, then tip-toed toward the garage.

Raynard lifted the garage door just enough to allow Ike's frail, fifteen-year-old body to slide in.

"Give it here," Ike said as his skinny arm poked out of the darkness.

Raynard gave Ike the container of lighter fluid, then looked to Pat's bedroom window as Ike's hand vanished into the shadows. A lightning bolt spider webbed across the sky, allowing Raynard to see Pat spying through the blinds. He shook his head as he waved, motioning for her to go away.

At sixteen, Raynard felt like he was light years ahead of Ike mentally. He had Ike doing the grunt work while he stood lookout. Raynard smiled at the warming thought of having both portions of the cash from cleaning Pat's basement safely at home. He could hear Ike inside the garage, sounding as if he were tripping over paint cans. His mind flashed to the day before.

He knew something was up. Pat was six years older than Raynard, but seemed to have a thing for him, always complimenting him on his broad shoulders or smooth, dark complexion. That time she had hired him to clean her basement the day before trash day with the promise of cashing him out the following day after she cashed her check. He never told Ike the payment arrangement when he enlisted him. He instead used his relation to Ike as a virgin to help reel him in for the task. "Yo, it's ol' girl with them bangin' hips and that big ass. She might let us fuck!"

Raynard had no intention of breaking a sweat, and definitely not with a sexy cougar like Pat on deck, so he offered Ike fifty of the planned one-fifty to help.

"Hell yeah," Ike said. "I think I can grab some Addidas with that!"

On payday morning, Raynard popped upright in bed at the sounds of birds chirping outside. He was amped at not only the thought of getting his money, but getting it from Pat.

He thought of how magical the wink was he received after finishing the job. It was better than any hug. It wasn't the normal closing and reopening of the eye, but more like the type of simple thing taken for granted until it had to be rehearsed dozens of times until the move was shaken free of all faults and added as a staple in some blockbuster film.

Raynard not only perceived the wink as a sign of Pat's attraction, but also as a reassurance that he would have exclusive rights to the business end of things. The graceful wink was most erotic to a sixteen-year-old looking to eradicate his virginity, but silent and secret as the financial amount that Ike would never know for sure.

Raynard surveyed his bedroom. He was almost certain that if he continued dwelling in the small crevice in his mom's vision he would soon succumb to claustrophobia. It was sufficient for a teen, but he was at the threshold of manhood.

He peeked at his pager to see if he had any beeps. That turned out to be just wishful thinking.

"Raynard," he heard his mother call.

Highly irritated by his mom's voice, Raynard rolled over in a cheap attempt at playing possum, hoping that she would leave him be. He was certain her call would mark the beginning of some daylong task that would interfere with his rendezvous with Pat.

Damn, he thought as his mom burst into his room.

"Boy, get yo lazy ass up outta that bed! It's damn near time for people to be gettin' off work and here yo' ass still sleep!" His mom's cigarette vapors quickly invaded his nostrils. "I need you to go to the store and get some rice for my salmon croquets."

Salmon croquets? Yeah boy! Raynard sat upright. *What a disgusting sight!* he thought as he watched his mom drop crumpled dollars onto his dresser. Her pink, foam rollers sectioned her hair while her open robe allowed peripherals of her dangling breasts.

After watching his door close, he leapt from his bed, remembering that in order to get to the store he would have to walk past Pat's street, where her house was conveniently the third from the corner, allowing him a clear view.

As he strolled down McNichols, Raynard decided to allow Pat time to page him. He tried with no avail to stroll by without even looking in the direction of her house. Daydreams of Pat standing on her porch waving him over caused him to glance repeatedly in her direction.

He slowed his pace in order to give Pat a few more minutes to get her mail, or cash her check, or finish whatever was keeping her from jangling his beeper.

At the store, Raynard wasted a few minutes listening to Tricky Rick and Fish Head Greg talk about one another. Rick and Greg were in their late twenties, and always had plastic cups in their hands, and were always posted at the liquor store hustling or just shooting their game at the females walking by.

"Ah, Raynard, my fifty-grand-man!" Tricky greeted Raynard. "Come on in and kick it with me and my protégé, puppy nuts." Tricky smoothly waved his left hand toward Gregg--Vanna White style. "That's a nice shirt that boy got on, ain't it, puppy nuts?"

"Nigga, fuck you," Fish Head told Tricky Rick.

Tricky Rick twisted his face in disgust. "Damn, is that yo' breath? That shit smell like ape turds rolled in newspaper!"

"Fool, I ain't gon' tell you no more to give Janet Jackson her shirt back!" Greg countered.

Raynard decided it was time to get back with the rice. He checked his pager once again before strolling slowly back home.

That time he noticed a car in Pat's driveway and figured it was her ride to go cash her check as he stopped on the curb to allow the mail truck to pass.

Halfway into his meal Raynard's pager vibrated in his pocket.

"Boy, you better not stop eating to get on the phone with them fast-tail gals!" his mother ordered. "I know one thang, you better do somethin' with that room up there before you end up stayin' in the basement!"

Raynard allowed the words to just roll right by him as he glanced at his pager's screen. It was Pat. *Fuck that basement!* he thought. *I got a bitch with her own crib*! He pushed away from the table and dashed up the stairs to his private quarters to converse in peace.

"Hey," Pat's voice sounded over the phone. "I got your money."

Raynard had no memory of hanging up the phone or even the trip to Pat's house. The next thing he knew he was standing on her porch. He could feel a boner coming on as his finger jabbed her doorbell.

Pat snatched the door open as if she were just as eager to see Raynard.

She was a goddess in a tee shirt and cutoff shorts. Her thick thighs squeezed from underneath the jean material.

"You gonna just stand there?" she asked, stepping to the side to allow him entry.

Raynard glanced at the interior of Pat's living room. It was simple, but nice. He doubted the females in his age bracket would have the taste or maturity to decorate the pad as Pat had. He had been barking up the wrong trees! But, finally he had struck gold. *I guess I'm still gon' have to go by and visit my mother sometimes!*

"Why you so quiet?" Pat asked, making eye contact.

"I'm just chillin'."

"You wanna have a cocktail with me?" Pat switched into the next room.

Raynard followed Pat into a den where he sat on a love seat between two fluffy pillows. As Pat stood in front of him he peeked through the gap where her legs met her crouch. He could feel his member beginning to stiffen.

She left the room and returned with two vodka and cranberries.

Raynard relaxed as they sat sipping. He had a beer before but never even thought about graduating to liquor. Over an hour had passed when he realized she had said nothing about his cash.

"So, what's up with the money?" he asked.

"Money?" she asked with a straight face.

"Yeah," he said in a serious tone, starting to feel as if he were about to get stiffed.

Pat stood, and then sat down her glass. She reached for Raynard's hand and helped him to his feet. "It's in my pocket but my shorts too tight." She sat her glass down and looked to Raynard.

"Okay, what you want me to do?" he asked, not knowing what to expect.

"You gon' have to get it yourself." Pat looked to Raynard with come-fuck-me eyes.

Raynard reached for her pocket as she moved closer and put her back to his chest.

Her soft buttocks ground against his concrete dick.

He started inside her pocket and instantly realized that there was plenty of room for a woman's small hands. Raynard could feel heat but no paper. He tried to go deeper, but soon ran out of the cotton material that composed her pockets. Instead, he was feeling a mat of coarse, curly hairs. *Her pussy!* he thought as he stroked her pubes.

This is it! It's about to go down! Raynard closed his eyes and placed his other arm around Pat's body, just below her breasts. He lightly polished her hairs with the fingertips of his buried hand. His blood simmered as Pat relaxed in his embrace.

Raynard's erection was full grown and he knew just what he wanted to do with it, but had no idea as to how to go about doing it. He didn't want to seem amateur to Pat so he tried to keep doing something to keep her from becoming bored with him. While his fingers probed as if reading Braille, he lowered his lips to her earlobes and flicked them lightly with his tongue. He remembered what his good buddy Dre told him in gym class about how to surely get the chicks wet, and lightly exhaled heated breaths into Pat's ear.

Pat ground her denimed buttocks back onto Raynard's stiffness, letting him know he was doing things right. She seized his wrist and pulled his hand from her pocket. Pat turned to face him. "What you tryin' to get started with yo' mannish self? Sit down for a minute." She pushed him back onto the loveseat and switched out of the room. She returned after a few minutes with a cup of ice.

"What you doin'? You tryin' to cool off or something?" Raynard asked.

Pat giggled. "No, I just wanna talk to you for a minute. That's all." She slid Raynard a folded wad of bills.

"Thanks." Raynard tried to hide his smile.

"I wanted to get that out of the way so you know it's not about money."

Awww shit, here we go! Raynard's dick throbbed and warmed his leg. He hoped that if it was time to do it she would just get undressed since he had no clue as to how he was supposed to get her out of her clothes.

"So, do you have a girlfriend?"

Raynard's mind went blank for an instant. Then, he remembered, Sue. They had been talking on the phone for the past year, but she lived so deep on the eastside of town that he never saw her. They had plans to go to prom together. There was also, Yolanda. She had been kind of flirty, but wouldn't let him get past a peck on the lips. He had been told by Tricky Rick that he would more than likely have to go to church with her for a while before he would get the chance to harpoon her. He wanted to smell his fingers right quick before he answered, but realized that that might make him seem perverted and get him thrown out. He knew Sue was supposed to be his girl, but she had no intention of letting him get down until after prom. That wouldn't happen for another two years. He shook his head no.

Pat drew closer and reached for Raynard's zipper.

Raynard mustered all of his strength in an effort to keep from smiling, but the left side of his mouth curved upward anyway as Pat yanked his button open and dropped his zipper. He felt charged with confidence as Pat taught him how to free the opposite sex of their clothes. He was ready to try until she pushed him back so that he was slouching in his seat. He didn't know what to expect.

Pat reached into Raynard's cotton trappings and stroked his meat until his eyes closed. She reached a bit lower and caressed his gonads with her fingertips.

The liquor and Pat's fondles had Raynard feeling as if he were floating through heaven. He dared not even lift an eyelid when he felt Pat lift up and settle on the floor between his legs. She continued to juggle his balls as he heard her crunching on the ice.

Nothing he had ever heard of could've prepared him for the hot breath on his dickhead immediately followed by the chill of the crushed ice. *Damn!* he thought.

He knew if Fish Head Greg or Tricky Rick or anyone had ever experienced anything remotely similar they would never stop talking about it. He knew he was the first ever! He had boasting rights that Ike would never understand. "Uungh," he sounded off as Pat's slurps caused his soul to blast out of his penis. He watched Pat continue to work until he went limp.

Raynard continued to sit in a slumped position--even kept his eyes closed as he heard Pat leave the room then return about ten minutes later. He felt her settle on the love seat next to him.

"What's on your mind?" Raynard asked.

"You wanna make a few more dollars?" Pat asked.

Wooed to the core by the sheepish look in Pat's eyes, Raynard said the only thing that made sense. "Hell yeah!"

"I kinda need help with somethin'."

Raynard was prepared to try nearly anything she could come up with. "What I gotta do?" he asked, more concerned with the look in her eyes than the dangers in her words.

Raynard watched and wondered just how he could possibly seal the deal and lock down a tender piece like Pat. He had touched her pubes so he knew she was hairy, and that turned him on. As Pat sat silent and frozen in thought for a moment, Raynard thought of how delightful it would've been to have found the *really* interesting part of her in that trap-door pocket than that field of nappy dreams, or to have even thought of it at the time.

As Pat told Raynard the importance of torching her garage during the upcoming thunderstorm, Raynard watched her lips and faint mustache dance with her words. He could only think of her beauty and how he would somehow have to be the man of her house.

"Okay, so remember, we need it to start like on the roof or somewhere up top so it look like it got struck by lightning," Pat said, looking at Raynard as if she hoped he would be following what she said.

"Need what to start?" Raynard asked, only catching a small portion of her instruction.

"The fire!" Pat twisted her lips. "I hope you payin' attention!"

"Oh, yeah! Hell yeah. I'm on it! I gotta start it on the roof." Raynard's mind was finally starting to process the crime Pat was asking him to commit. He knew it was wrong, but had no idea how wrong. He really didn't even care.

"Do you got somebody to help you to make sure you do it right?"

"I got it," Raynard assured with his chest poked out.

"No, look at me." Pat gave him a look of sincerity and hopefulness. "I need this to go right so we get paid, baby."

"Oh, I'm your baby now?" Raynard asked with a blush.

"You better be!" Pat stood and waited for Raynard to get to his feet. "Do you got somebody you can trust to keep quiet?"

"Yup. I can get my homeboy, Ike." Raynard said, still questioning in his own mind whether or not Ike would keep his mouth closed.

"Cool, baby!" Pat wrapped Raynard in her arms and squeezed him. "I'll throw you one-fifty. It's on you how much you give your boy."

I guess if it's up to me that nigga ain't gotta get shit! He talk too much anyway. I might not even tell him about--naw, fuck that! I gotta talk some shit about that ice! Raynard quickly grabbed Pat in an embrace as she released him. He tried slipping his hand back in her pocket.

Pat seized his fingers. "Don't even try it. Maybe later. We gotta take care of this business first. Go dig up your friend." She slapped him on the rear on his way out.

The clap of thunder snapped Raynard out of his trance. He turned to the window to see if Pat had seen the way he jumped when startled. He didn't see her, but knew she was somewhere still peeking.

The garage door squeaked then flew open. Raynard backed up a few steps to allow Ike an exit. The two ran thru the open gate back into the alley from which they came.

"We got that bitch!" Ike said with spunk as he and Raynard smoked a joint while walking down Strathmoor toward Pat's house where there was a crowd and fire trucks.

They scanned the crowd looking for Pat.

Ike stepped close to Raynard. "I see her over by Troy."

Raynard looked to see Pat. For a brief moment he marveled at the way the red light from the fire truck illuminated her loveliness.

She shot him a dick solidifying smile.

Playing things off, Raynard turned to Ike. "Yup, that's her!"

"Yeah. Her dumb ass over there smilin' cause she think she got down on us! Bitch!"

Raynard laughed with Ike. Raynard then began laughing to himself at Ike while trying to figure out a way to fade away from him.

"Sinbad comin'!" someone shouted from the crowd, announcing the presence of the Harrison's wolf dog.

"Quick!" Raynard said to Ike in a loud whisper. "Let's follow them!" Raynard pointed in the direction of the crowd headed toward McNichols. He watched Ike start off with the rest as he followed Pat into her side door.

Raynard woke to blinding lights. He was heaving as if he had just ran up a flight of a hundred stairs, or had been holding his breath nearly too long. A quick look around the room made him remember the test.

"How do you feel?" asked the familiar voice of Lenard as he stepped into Raynard's view.

Raynard tried to reach to rub his nose but felt the straps holding him to the chair. His nose needed rubbing even more since he knew he was restrained.

"Take these straps loose!" Raynard yelled. The sobering reality began to set in. The new drug was wearing off and he was getting irritable. Even worse, he'd been given a dose of something that sent him back to the good old days. Back when things were best in his life. Back when Pat was a young, bad bitch full of game and slick schemes to make quick bankrolls. She always had something going on back then. Much of what she learned came from the street players with lightening fast wits and long bankrolls.

Pat had a stunning figure as long as Raynard could ever remember seeing her around in the 'hood. He knew she had to have been propositioned with everything from cash to the Eiffel Tower for a slice of that ass before she gave him a chance. But now, whatever he had was wearing off fast.

Raynard reached into his underwear to see if he'd just had a wet dream. They were dry. He remembered that he was just helping with the experimental project, and didn't even pay for the blow he'd been given. "Yo, let me get one of those for the road," he asked Lenard.

"I can't do it!" Lenard said with no hesitation. "You see we gotta have you strapped in when we give it to you here. It's a reason for that."

Raynard didn't give a damn what the reason, he wanted another blow. That new stuff had him feeling better than anything he ever tried, plus he had the best sex he'd had in a long time. He knew he had no argument that could contend with the strap situation, so he decided not to even try to buy any. He instead figured he would wait until his services were needed again, then he would try to get something extra.

He sniffed, then wiped his nose on his way out, looking back for any sign saying he might be eligible for another get-high at that time.

CHAPTER 2

Raynard woke with his member rock hard. He knew he was with Pat, the same woman he'd had so much pleasure with the night before, but this was her present self. The disgusting, bloated Pat. Over the years she became an alcoholic beast who could inhale a half-dozen Krispy Kremes before he could make a twelve minute trek to the corner store.

He looked over, slowly shaking his head at her heavy wheezing while she lay on her side with her back to him. He knew well that whenever she rolled onto her back those wheezes graduated to bass-filled snores.

Raynard reached over and pulled the covers off her, then tried to roll her over. He never really realized how inflated the row of rolls covering her body had become until then. *How and when exactly did she let herself go?* he asked himself as if he had not been there watching the gradual change firsthand.

"Uhh-unnn," she moaned in dismay as he struggled to roll her over. She loved sex, but he first had to get her out of her liquor-induced coma.

He hastily flung the cover to the floor as he pulled one of her legs away from the other. He then looked down and could barely see her nappy patch beneath her overlapping stomach. He knew it had to be something in that drug keeping his dick stiff, because it sure wasn't her. He had just hit her a week ago, but now, after being with her *youthful* self, he dreaded having to lie on top of her huge gut in order to enter her. But, he had to do something with his morning wood.

"Lift up," he told her as he slid a pillow under her butt in an attempt to make her stomach roll back some. Disappointed, because that only put her higher up, he snatched the pillow and flung it on top of the cover he had tossed minutes earlier.

Unable to just rest on top of her, he rested in the push-up position looking down at her. He knew once she was waked she would welcome his hard dick. Somehow he nearly got an attitude as she reached down and felt his stiffness. She smiled as she navigated his beast into her crevice. He injected her with her morning blessing and pumped hard. Raynard wanted to slap her hands away as she rubbed his back and arms while moaning in delight. He just pumped harder and faster. She raised her legs high and kept them there, something she hadn't done in a long time.

Whatever he had taken had him harder than he had been in ages, and though he felt Pat was now a disgusting blob, her pussy felt wonderful. He could feel everything inside her as he stroked and stretched her like he had when he was a younger man.

She gripped his shoulder and pulled him closer to her as she began to buck her hips more violently. Unable to escape, Raynard had no choice but continue to bang her out. He was now growing tired of the act and wanted to cum, but wasn't there yet.

As he continued to stroke, he closed his eyes and flashed back to the night before. He had forgotten how beautifully curvaceous Pat was back then. It was so easy to get to her pussy once he climbed on top of her. And when he put it in, he knew he was home. Her response was quite different back then. Then, she sounded off from the time he entered her, to the time he completed the job.

The thoughts of her kittenish vajay-jay had him nearing his climax. He bit his lip and locked her legs back with his arms as his hands rested on her shoulders, pinning her to the bed. "It's too deep, it's too deep!" she wailed as he bottomed her out. He felt like he was getting some get-back for her mood being stuck on bitch as he felt his dick seem to get bigger and harder as he came.

"What the hell you done had?" she asked with dreamy eyes and a wide grin as he got off of her.

He ignored her completely and went into the bathroom to clean up. He didn't give a damn if she got mad. He didn't want to be bothered with her anyway. He just wanted to get into the streets to find more of what had him in ecstasy the night before.

* * *

Raynard peeked through the blinds of their living room window. It was beginning to get dark and he heard nothing from his old buddy, Ike, or their mutual friend, Lenard, who introduced him to the new experimental high. He was starting to fiend for another blow, especially if it meant he would again get to revisit his past.

Ever since he had got his rocks off that morning, he had been daydreaming of Pat in her youth. He couldn't help but wonder if he would get to go back there with her every time he took the new drug. If that was going to be the case, he knew he was going to go broke chasing the high.

The one thing Raynard knew for sure was that Pat had not faked feeling him that morning, and ever since she had been trailing him around, speaking in the sweetest tones. Not a single smart remark slipped from her lips since he got off her, and that was a record. She would normally sit in front of the television watching some stupid reality or talk show, shushing him whenever he tried to speak to her unless it was a commercial break.

Raynard sat on the couch and checked to make sure the ringer was on on his cell phone. He could hear the toilet flush, then heard water running in the sink. He knew his few minutes of peace were over. The floorboards cracked, creaked and popped under the strain of her weight. Raynard rested his elbow on the edge of the couch, then propped his chin up with his fist. Closing his eyes, he tried to fake like he was asleep.

He felt the couch next to him sink as Pat settled in. "You sleep already?" she asked as she pushed his shoulder.

He turned toward her. "If you thought I was sleep, why would you push me?" he questioned, careful not to get too snappy since she was in a good mood for a change.

She shrugged her shoulders and reached for his zipper. "Maybe I was thinkin' 'bout all that good lovin' you gave me this mornin'."

Raynard looked at her and could hardly believe she was being so peaceful. Normally, they would be arguing at that time of the day. They beefed and bickered constantly over *something*, at least until she began gettin' her sip on. Then, she would be smooth until she neared the end of her second half-pint. By that time, she would get tough as the rib tips under the heat lamp in the corner liquor store. It was that type of behavior that had him hating her, because he felt like he *could* have a happy relationship with a big girl, but Pat just didn't seem to like or respect him anymore. She was always short with him, and could get cold as the other side of his pillow. He constantly prayed for peace so he could at least enjoy himself when he got his buzz on, but never thought that peace would come based on his sexual performance.

Pat had worked her way into his zipper and began creeping into his boxers when Raynard gripped her wrist and asked, "Can I at least get us some food first? You know we can't do nothin' on a empty stomach."

Pat sat upright and removed her hand from his pants. "For real, tell me, did you take somethin' to make you hard like that earlier?"

"I will tell you when I get back."

She sucked her teeth and twisted her lips, obviously trying to let him know she had some idea what he might've been up to. "You just wanna go get a blow! Why you always gotta get high?"

"Same reason you always gotta drink!" he countered, trying to heat things up so he could play mad and storm out of the house.

Pat took a deep breath and looked at him. "Can you at least do it again?"

"What?" he snapped. Looking in her eyes, he cooled down fast. She sincerely wanted to get banged out again. He knew he just didn't have it in him. He wasn't at all turned on by her, especially after gettin' it on with her younger self.

He knew he had to dip out and try to find more of the good stuff in order to help them both. "What you want to eat?"

"Whatever you get."

He looked back at Pat's shaking head as he left out the door.

CHAPTER 3

Raynard whipped his small Grand Prix through his 'hood in the McNichols and Schaefer area looking for any signs of Lenard or Ike, hoping to get the same effect that he had the night before. He usually considered the boundaries of his 'hood to be about a square mile, but under his current circumstances he increased the size about three to four blocks in every direction; going slow down every block, and even slower when crossing side streets, hoping to run into his connect.

He sat at the stop sign on Stansbury at Puritan, trippin' because he knew last night was way more than just a dream. He had all kinds of dreams in his forty years on the planet, but none was ever so vivid and memorable as that one. He could almost feel her rough pubes on his fingertips.

He was shaken out of his trance by some jackoff leaning on his horn in the car behind him. He never even knew the traffic cleared. He began easing across Puritan, then looked in his rear-view. It was Mel, a guy he had gone to Cerveny Middle School with.

Mel was cool, but Raynard considered himself a much better man than Mel since Mel did Heroin, and he only snorted girl. Mel was good to know because when the drought season hit, Mel was *still* getting high. Even in times when the most decorated street veteran couldn't find a connect, Mel was gettin' down.

Raynard stomped his brake, then twirled his steering wheel all the way right, almost hitting oncoming traffic as he tailed Mel. He figured if he couldn't find Ike or Lenard, he might possibly be able to find another connect on the new drug.

He could see Mel eyeballing him from his rear-view as Raynard closed in, pulling close to Mel's bumper after following him into the gas station on Schaefer.

Mel hopped out and walked back to Raynard's car with an irritated look on his face. "What up, Ray?" he asked Raynard.

Raynard sniffed. "Hey, what's up, bro? You seen Lenard and 'em?" Raynard watched Mel's face closely.

"Naw, but what you tryin' to do? You need a one-on-one?" Mel asked, talking bag talk.

"You got them same blows ol' boy got?" Raynard knew it was a slim chance that even Mel could deliver on that request.

"Yeah, man. You know me, baby!" Mel's face reflected irritation. "Shit, I'm here to meet my man right here." Mel pointed to a raggedy, brown van with a red driver's side door.

Raynard watched as Mel stepped over and got into the van. He came back after a few minutes with something cupped in his hands. Raynard nearly got excited thinking that Mel could possibly have had a handful of the new blows.

Mel walked over to Raynard's passenger door. Raynard very quickly popped the locks.

Mel's fist held Raynard's full attention. "What's the business?" Raynard asked. He watched as Mel slowly opened his hand, revealing four white sticks with square heads, each a different color, and each wrapped in clear plastic. "Suckers?"

"Naw, man. Morphine lollipops. Ol' boy got a bag of 'em!"

"What the fuck? I don't do that shit. I fuck with the pow-wow. All I want is them new blows."

"I know," Mel began, pointing a lollipop at Raynard. "That nigga, Ike, you lookin' for…Ike like to do diesel."

"Ike?" Raynard asked in amazement. He'd known Ike forever and doubted anyone could've told him anything he didn't already know about him.

"Yeah. I see him at the spot on Freeland all the time. And this morphine ain't nothin' but just like heroin." Mel shook his head a few times then continued. "Yeah, just get these lollipops, then trade 'em for what you want."

Raynard thought for a moment. "How I know he gon' want that shit. I ain't never even heard of no morphine lollipops! I'll be stuck with that bullshit!"

"Naw, bro. I ain't gon' play you like that! Look, dopefiends suck on these for a li'l while, then get to noddin'. They can't even finish a whole sucker before they head drop. It do 'em better than a regular blow. Only thang is, they can't find these. *He* only got these 'cause after his cousin Bo died from Cancer, he broke in the house to steal the rest of his shit."

This nigga might be on ta somethin'! "How much?"

"Ten. Four for thirty-five."

Knowing he only had thirty bucks in his pocket, Raynard said, "Two for fifteen!"

"Damn! You don't wanna see me make shit, do you? Can I eat with you sometimes?" Mel complained, but quickly dropped the suckers into Raynard's hand as he snatched the cash.

As soon as the passenger door slammed and Mel began to step away, Raynard felt like he'd been had. He didn't know for sure if Ike was using heroin, and didn't know if he was going to even see Ike. He still had the money for Pat's food, but planned to come up with a slick excuse if she asked about his. He knew he wouldn't have to even pay for the blows once he found Ike, but planned to use the lollipops to trade for a little take-home snort. He figured Ike would be in a bargaining mood once he got wind of the fact that he had lollipops.

*   *   *

Raynard pulled to the empty parking spot in front of the liquor store he visited in his buzzed time the night before. He stopped and looked around, remembering the differences in the area. Decades had past, yet he was able to see everything so clearly while he was blowed the night before. The little knick-knack things he never even paid attention to like the abandoned cleaners at the corner of Mark Twain. The night before, it was in business as he walked down the ave in search of Pat and his fee. The bar next door which was Teresa's Place was called the Boardroom back then and even the liquor store he was in front of was black owned way back and called Doris Ann's.

The liquor store, he remembered, thinking of Fish Head and Tricky. He knew they would be able to point him in the right direction.

"Raynard," Tricky Rick shouted as soon as Raynard entered the store. "My fifty-grand-man!"

"Damn. Yesterday I was yo' hundred-grand-man!"

"Fifty! Fifty grand, my nigga! You gotta work yo' way up to a hundred," Tricky assured. Tricky

Rick had on fresh kicks with new Levi's. His shirt was even new—a crispy tee, argyle printed with the Polo dude atop his steed—something the dope boys had yet to get a hold of. He was amped like he was high as he wanted to be. He stood in aisle four, leaning back, doing a dance that looked like he was turning bike pedals backwards with his hands while pumping his hips.

Raynard was trippin' for a minute thinking of how long Tricky Rick had been doing and saying the same stuff like calling him his fifty-grand-man, and was really tripping over the fact that Tricky was bustin' fresh when, up until a few days earlier, he was wearing gear that Raynard wouldn't cut grass in.

Fish Head Greg, sitting on the ice cream freezer, began to lift his head from a lofty nod. He looked at Raynard and flashed a makeshift smile before his chin dove back to the middle of his chest. A stream of slobber escaped his bottom lip and began to pool between his manboobs.

Raynard walked to the counter and ordered a half-pint of Pat's favorite Vodka, then headed for the door.

As his fingertips touched the door's handle, he looked back to see Greg smiling while still in his nod. Greg's mouth drooped into a dopefiend frown, then the left side of his mouth curled upward. He held that expression for a moment before graduating to a full-blown smile. A missing bicuspid showed like an open window.

Noticing Raynard's fascination with Greg, Tricky said, "Oh yea, dog nuts goin' through it right now!"

"He's not puppy nuts no more?" Raynard asked, thinking of his own high from the day before.

"Damn! I ain't been able to call him puppy nuts in a long time. That was back when he just 'ooted dogfood. He a vet now when it come to doin' heroin. If he didn't *really* have a fish head, niggas would probly call him pin cushion for all the needles he jab in his ass. Yeah, he dog nuts for sure these days!" Tricky began sending a text before saying, "Yeah, he probly cruisin' memory lane so tough right about now..."

Tricky's statement caught Raynard's full attention. "Memory lane? What?"

Tricky Rick playfully jabbed at Raynard's gut while saying, "You know what I'm talkin' bout. I heard you be at the joint where Ike and 'em be."

"Ike? You seen him? Where he at?"

"Hold on playa! You was just with him yesterday. He must not *want* you to know where he is."

"Whats up with them blows he got?" Raynard wanted to know.

It ain't the blows, fool. It's the cut. I got some. Wanna blow?"

Raynard almost felt disrespected for Tricky to try to sell him a bag of heroin when its effects were clearly being displayed by Fish Head, who was grinning and drooling so shamelessly with his large eyes spinning and twirling under their lids.

"Nigga, you know I don't fuck with that shit!"

"I know, but it got that cut on it. You can be the new puppy nuts!"

Raynard's patience was nearly non-existent at that point. "Man, where Ike and 'em at?"

"Don't know," Tricky began, walking away as if Raynard no longer deserved his company. "Call him."

Raynard left the store pissed, actually mad at Tricky because he felt like Tricky knew where Ike was, but was just hatin' for one reason or another.

Raynard hopped in his car and jetted from the curb, back on his mission to deliver Pat's grub.

As he rode down Freeland, Raynard saw the brown van from earlier. *Mel!* he thought, whipping into the alley just before Fenkell that led into the parking lot of Onassis Coney Island. He poked the Coney number into his phone, made Pat's order, then sat back to scope out the scene.

Raynard watched as the van Mel rode in backed into a parking spot at the far end of the lot, on the other side of the alley. Mel hopped out, then the driver. Mel's extreme pimp walk let Raynard know Mel was excited, but the way Mel walked way faster than the guy he was with let Raynard know Mel wanted to make it to some dope before his counterpart.

"Psst," Raynard sounded.

Mel turned and when he saw Raynard, he gave the "aww, him again?" face. But, quickly stepped over to him. "What's poppin'?"

"Where you headed?" Raynard inquired.

"Shit, man. Guess we found your mans and 'em."

"Who?" Raynard asked playing dumb. He was so anxious he wanted to hear Mel say it.

"Ike."

Raynard gasped, as in such disbelief.

"Yeah, man. He over in that building across the street where Bo-Jays used to be. Alright, I gotta get! From the looks of that line them niggas must be givin' out testers!" Mel turned and walked away fast.

When Raynard went in to get Pat's food, he looked across the street and saw what looked like everyone in the area who ever experimented with drugs. He snatched the food and ran to the car. He stomped the gas. He now knew where he wanted to be.

* * *

Raynard looked around once he got in the house. No lights were on and Pat had candles burning all over the place. She walked into the living room wearing something red and see-through. She had taken the time to do something sexy to her hair and even had perfumed scents going up his nose.

"What took so long?" she asked in a sweet voice. The sweetest he'd heard in a while. As she got closer he could even tell by the whisky breath that she had started on a bottle.

Raynard had seen plenty of days when that smell on her breath meant he had to duck, but on that particular day, he knew she wanted him to stretch up in her past the Viagra zone, to where only true romance could stiffen and lengthen his pipe to reach and widen enough for penile veins to leave erotic imprints on her cave walls.

"Had to give one of my partners a ride to the east side." he lied.

"Where yo' food at?" she asked in a way that made him feel like he may have to tussle over the carry-out box in his hands if he planned to claim it as his own.

"Aw, shit," he began. "I didn't grab nothin' yet 'cause I knew I was gonna have to dash back out and wouldn't get a chance to eat it now. I'm just gon' grab somethin' in a li'l while when I get done runnin'. You know I hate my shit cold!" he said, as if she would understand.

Pat's face went blank with an inhale. As she exhaled, her face expressed disgust. "Baby, you need to leave that bullshit alone. How can you fuck with somethin' that's gon' keep you from eatin'?

That shit kill your appetite and you just keep gettin' skinny!"

Already cranky and irritated by the monkey on his back, Raynard blurted out, "Man, I'm straight! Damn!" His face quickly softened as he tried to clean things up with, "I feel you, and I'm blessed to have you on my side, but really, I'm cool." He turned and headed for the door.

"Fuckin' dopefiend!"

CHAPTER 4

Raynard blew through three stop signs along with a slew of traffic violations as he made it back to where he had seen Mel. Heading south on Fenkell at breakneck speeds, he nearly tipped the small car making a right onto Freeland. His heart quickly sank when he looked across the street and saw only deserted storefronts.

He got out of the car and stepped toward the dumpster at the far end of the parking lot. He could hear voices near and remembered the winos that usually made camp behind Sam's Liquor store. He planned to shakedown every one of them with hopes of finding where the party from earlier had gone.

As he took a wiz in the ghetto latrine, Raynard realized that there were no winos behind the liquor store, and the voices were just a tad bit fainter than before. He headed back to the car when the voices got louder again. He walked past the car and stopped on the Fenkell sidewalk. He looked left toward Ardmore and saw that cars were parked along both sides of that street, on the block going south of Fenkell. Two gritty-looking dudes hopped out of a cab and quickly sprinted in the direction of the alley that ran behind the building where Raynard had seen the long line earlier. Reasoning that things must have gotten out of hand to the point that the mob had to be redirected to the rear; Raynard raced toward the voices, toward the good blows, toward a time when Pat's pussy was pristine, toward the good times.

Raynard got to the alley and saw a procession that rivaled the cheese line outside Focus Hope in the eighties, during Reaganomics. There was no way he was going to be a part of that circus, so he started past the clowns standing, waiting their turn. As he walked he could hear all kinds of sniffs, snorts, and sinus clearing noises.

"I don't know where you goin'!" he heard a male voice say.

"Maybe the nigga work here," said another.

"Shit, all I know is he ain't gettin' in front of me," said the first voice before a sniff.

Raynard reached the door where the line seemed to tighten as if everyone in it suspected him of having plans to cut in front. A Herculean goon with folded arms guarded the door. Raynard didn't recognize him from the 'hood, but knew as long as he dropped the names of those he was close to, he would be held in high regard.

"Where the fuck you think you goin'?" asked the goon. His demeanor and the tones in which he spoke suggested that he had been kept in a dark basement for the majority of his life and fed only hot sauce.

"What up, cuz?" Raynard began. With no response to his greeting, he sniffed, then continued with, "Yea, I'm here for my man, Ike. He here?"

"Did you call him?"

"He said meet him back here."

"Oh, well, I guess you already got that worked out. Meet him back here, but don't get too close to me." The goon was as empathetic as a rattlesnake with missed-meal cramps. "Next," said the goon to the lucky 'fiend in the front of the line.

The goon pressed the button on the headset over his left ear. He then opened the door and let the skeletal 'fiend in. For the brief moment while the door was opened, Raynard goose necked and peeked, trying to find an explanation for why he was outside when his peoples ran the whole operation.

Raynard saw white lab coats moving around chairs, and was pretty sure he had seen Ike in there calling shots, and for that matter, he even thought he saw a chick making rounds holding an hors d'oeuvres tray with exposed mammaries.

"Yo, that's him!" Raynard shouted as he advanced before being stiff armed.

"Dude, you crowdin' me over here!" spat the goon. "Get yo' ass to the back!"

"I keep tellin' you Ike an 'em is my mans! Why you ain't ask him?"

"Look, bruh. You just told me you talked to the nigga on the phone. Why do I gotta say anything to him if you just talked to him and he s'posed to be meetin' yo' ass back here? I'm just doin' my job that I need to feed my kids, so, get the fuck to the back until you talk to him again." The goon took the pose of an action figure, ready to smash Raynard at the next blink.

Raynard quickly read the goons stance and started toward the rear, wishing he knew Karate or something.

By the time Raynard found the end of the line, it had crossed Ardmore and was behind Morris Hardware on the next block. He stood there behind a skinny white male with a rural haircut. In Raynard's 'hood they called it a "Timmy", and it looked like someone just dropped a bowl on his head and cut around it. He also had a skull tattooed on each of his temples. He called himself Pitbull, but was dubbed by the media as "The Cash Register Bandit." He spun wild heist tales to the unfortunate soul in front of him.

After a few minutes of standing, Raynard finally moved up three steps. By that time, Cappy and his crew stepped in line behind Raynard. Cappy was tall and lanky and always wore a fisherman's hat. He was somewhere in his sixties, but was known by every generation of Cooley Cardinal for posting up at the fruit market on Hubble at Fenkell. Later in the evening he would post at Be-Bee's gas station on Strathmoor, and if you refused his gas pumping services, he may just reach into his old-school bag of obscenities and call you a, "Jive turkey!" He could always be found cruising the 'hood on his ancient ten-speed bike. It had the handlebars from the seventies that curved downward in half-circles.

On that particular night, however, Cappy was on foot with his two compadres. One was an inch taller than he, and the other was a short guy, about four-eleven, with a forty-ounce wrapped in his sausage link fingers.

Shorty had more interesting heist tales than the cash register bandit, or it could have been that he just told his tales better, but he boasted about robbing Federal's Department Store back in the day on McNichols and Schaefer, next to the Mercury Movie Theatre.

"You remember that shit don'tcha, Cappy?" Shorty said. "You remember how we used to just roll in and—pow—put a bullet in the ceilin' to get them fools attention before layin' they asses down..."

Cappy had been eyeballin' a slim strawberry a few heads behind him, and seemed to be tired of hearing Shorty's stories before they even walked up. "Don't know 'bout all that, but I 'member yo' freaky ass got kicked off Belle Isle for sniffin' them girls bicycle seats!"

Everyone from the strawberry to the cash register bandit got off on Cappy's punchline.

"Aw, man!" said Shorty. With no defense, he simply turned up his forty-ounce.

Cappy must've felt guilty knowing that in a single sentence he had exposed Shorty's freaky side and took him from notorious heist man to a perv, booted from a public park. He simply laid a hand on Shorty's shoulder and said, "You know you my mellow."

Raynard reached the point where he was finally sixth in line when he noticed the door easing open. Lenard's head peeped out, then ducked back in. That had Raynard much more vigilant, and he glued his eyes to that door until Lenard jumped from the crack in it five minutes later.

"Psst!" sounded Raynard. He knew Lenard heard him. He also knew the goon had heard him, and was giving the evil eye. Raynard watched as Lenard stepped to the side of the door and fired up a cig. *I'm just gon' wait til' he finish smokin' to holla at him,* thought Raynard.

"Hey, can I get shorts on that square?" asked the man in front of the cash register bandit.

The goon unfolded his arms and said, "No!"

Raynard felt like his chances were blown since the goon would now be even more watchful of the thirsty 'fiends. Then he remembered..., "Lenard!" he shouted. He was on a first-name-basis.

The goon pointed a forefinger of warning Raynard's way.

Lenard looked in Raynard's direction. "Who's there?"

"It's me, Ray!" He spoke freely since he was addressed and saw that the goon was standing down. "Raynard, from last night."

"Oh, hi." stated Lenard as he simply walked back into the light-filled room on the other side of the door.

"That ho-ass nigga!" Raynard said, careful to let those in line with him hear, but not the goon.

"Yeah, that's how they get," Cappy began. "Soon as they get to shakin' that bag, they don't know you no mo'. Just forget about all the dog shit you done cleaned outta they yard for pennies to keep they mammy's foot outta they ass. Yes, sir, that bag is somethin' else!"

Raynard felt Cappy's words, but felt too regal to admit it. He was beginning to get more irritable thinking of being turned around when cracking for a free blow. He was penniless with some suckers, and wasn't even sure if Ike was even down with that program.

"Shit," started the cash register bandit. "We just fuck niggas like that up in my 'hood, out in Mt. Clemens."

Mt. Clemens? thought Raynard. He couldn't guess how word of the new dope could have travelled so fast, but figured the trailer parks of Macomb County were a fine place for the bandit to unleash his wrath.

Things got kind of quiet in Raynard's area of the line as they got closer to the door, but on the other side of Cappy, he could hear someone say, "...Yea, I did some last night, and it had me back when I was hangin' out at the Tender Trap downtown. Man, I was sharp as them mouse turds in your Cornflakes! Had on my black Bossalini, and shit, my shoes was like two hundred a heel even back then!"

"Next," Raynard heard the goon say.

He shuffled toward the door, trying to yank it as the goon slowly moved it open while daring Raynard with his eyes. Raynard just released the door and let him have his last few seconds of being in charge.

After the goon was done exacting his petty torments, Raynard jumped into the room, scanning the place for Ike.

"Raynard," he heard Ike's voice say from behind him. Ike was leaning on a steel table behind the door. He looked tired.

"What it do? Man, y'all had me out there for about a hour!"

"*Who* had you out there?" Ike asked.

"You know what I mean. Y'all didn't tell me to come, but…"

"Shit, I been busy as hell! You see how crazy this shit is. Like you said, it's the recipe."

"Yup. That's right!" Raynard said. "Shit, man, what up? Y'all still need my help right?"

"For what?" Ike asked, taking a complete trip to nutsville.

"Like yesterday." Raynard watched with hopeful eyes, but knew inside he had nothing coming.

"Man, you see that shit out there? We gon' need help with more security if anything."

"Well, shit, I got these morphine lollipops! Let's do a trade!" Raynard began rubbing his hands together.

"Man, I got a bag of them already. I got all kinda shit, man. I need that cash!"

Raynard sniffed. "I'm kinda strapped right now. Look out for ya mans." Raynard could see in Ike's eyes that he may have a bag coming if he could just come with some spontaneously funny kind of stuff that he was so good at. But, his yearn for the dope smothered his creative skills and the best he could muster was, "Come on, playa! I was y'all first guinea pig!" which seemed to make Ike's mouth curve upward on one side--but not even a smile.

Ike stuck two fingers into the pocket of his white lab coat and pulled out a small plastic bag, twisted and melted closed at the end.

Raynard sniffed then asked, "Well, shit, what about having to be strapped in and shit?"

"At first, we didn't know if we would have people going through convulsions, or seizures, or what. Now, we know just what we workin' with."

"Thanks to me, huh?" Raynard said, in a tone suggesting that he might be owed a little something.

"I guess, kinda, sorta. Oh, don't forget my suckers," said Ike with a plunderous grin.

Raynard walked back to his car, oblivious to the infantry of waiting customers. *That nigga knew I was comin' back just like he knew I was wastin' my time in that fuckin' line. That's why he had the shit ready!* Raynard thought, wishing Ike a month in Hell for yo-yoing with him.

CHAPTER 5

Raynard noticed the low-hanging, full moon as he tripped up the three stairs to his porch. He finally copped, and better yet, he was geeked to be able to do his blow in the privacy of his own home. He prayed for another high like he had before where he slipped into the past, but had no idea how things would pan out with Pat being so horny.

He opened the front door, holding his other hand behind him to keep the screen door from slamming, and eased into the house. *Yes!* he thought as he noticed Pat passed out on the couch. He had no idea how much she drank, but knew it had to be at least a pint from the way she snored. With one leg on the couch and the other resting on the floor, her red nightie was raised high enough to expose her vulva. He had no interest in finding out how it got that way, but could only imagine the huge caliber slug he ducked by spending so much time in line.

Raynard shucked his clothes and left them in a heap in the middle of the floor. He knew Pat would have a fit, but figured they would serve as an alarm as she tripped over them coming in. He even left his phone on top of his clothes because he didn't want any interruptions if he managed to flash back and get it on with the youthful Pat.

Raynard dove into the bed with the blow in hand. As he rested on his pillow, he began unraveling the small package, careful not to spill a grain. With the end melted closed, he knew he would more than likely have to rip a hole in the plastic, so he sat up.

He reached for the autographed cd on the nightstand he got from Payroll of the Cashout Doughboys. He laid the cd down on the bed and lightly ripped the blow open. He sprinkled the powder onto the cd, shaped the dope into a line using his forefinger, then sniffed and snorted until he saw no more powder. He licked his finger, then swabbed the cd with his tongue. He looked to the plastic that had contained the dope and saw eentsy-weentsy traces of white, so he licked and sucked the wrapper clean, not wanting to leave anything behind since he had no idea where the magic lay when it came to the new blows.

*　　　　　*　　　　　*

Raynard stood on the corner of Hubble and McNichols waiting on the bus. It seemed to be early and he was freezing his nuts off. He immediately saw Mike Mo riding past in an eighty-eight Taurus. Mike saw him and immediately stopped.

"How far you goin'?" Mike asked.

"Redford, I guess," Raynard said without a thought, but realized if he was at that particular bus stop at that time of the day, Redford High was the only place he could've been headed. He got in and thought, *Oh, shit! I know I'm back 'cause Mike had a stroke in the late nineties and can't even drive no more!*

"You guess? You don't sound too much like you really wanna go to school."

Raynard looked over at Mike, knowing he was right. He didn't want to go to school. He just wanted to see Pat.

"You guess! Ha ha! I remember them, 'I guess' days. That's one of the ways I ended up in the street. If I could do it all again knowing what I know now, man, shiiit! I would be so straight."

Raynard felt like he was hit with a lightning bolt. He felt what Mike was saying and knew he was living his chance to go back again, knowing what he knew as his older, mature self.

Mike had been around hustling since before Y.B.I or any of the crack giants whose stories were told in documentaries, and he always sprinkled Raynard with game to sharpen his hustle.

Raynard looked over at Mike. "So, what would you do?"

"That's a good question. I would really have to think about which way I would go, 'cause it's so many opportunities I passed up. For one, I wouldn't get high."

"You mean you wouldn't smoke weed?"

"Weed, liquor, coke, nothin'."

Raynard never even knew Mike messed around with anything but weed.

"I see you lookin' all crazy. Yea, I did a li'l powder here and there. Not that crack shit."

Raynard sat alert as a deer in a beam of headlamps.

"See, when I was comin' up, 'cain was a luxury drug. Only niggas with money did it. That was powder. Everybody on the 'up' snorted a li'l bit. Shit, we was makin' more than a lot of them niggas at Motown. And, I know for sure 'cause so many of 'em came around here to cop. I mean, can you imagine makin' twenty-five hundred in a day?"

Raynard knew he had seen a few of those days, but Mike was talking to someone of high school age, so he played the part. "Naw, not right now. Maybe in a year—"

"Yeah, but that's what I'm tellin' you, we was doin' it almost every day back in the seventies and eighties. Nobody wasn't worried about gettin' hooked on 'cain. We made that bread, then popped a few bottles. You gotta have some bad bitches, or it really ain't no party. I'm tellin' you, a line or two bring the three-way out a bitch!"

Raynard smiled knowing the words Mike spoke were true. He'd had some of the best times of his life building his coke habit up to where it was.

"Yeah, but see, all that sound like fun, but it ain't even worth it. I wouldn't even smoke weed or drink. Drugs are made to be sold. All that shit just hold you back in life. Think about that weed you sellin'; look at what one of your regular customers spend with you a week. Now, think of what that look like in a month, or better yet, a year."

Now Raynard thought of his habit with a frown. *I done sniffed a lotta brother's pockets fat!* Then he realized, *Damn, my nose ain't ran in a long time!*

To be sure of the era, Raynard checked his waist for his beeper. *I got my Ram!* He knew he was in business. He checked his pockets and pulled out Ziplock baggies filled with weed. He slid Mike one.

"This me?" asked Mike.

"Yeah. For the ride."

"Aw, shit. You know I wouldn't charge you."

"Naw, take it. It's yours! Matter 'o fact…" Raynard reached into his pocket and yanked out two more bags. "Take these!" he told him, thinking of how cool he had always been to him even before having a stroke.

"Damn!" Mike said. "You musta been doin' somethin' right lately. But, see," Mike began, holding one of the bags as they crossed Evergreen. "You need to tear off all this excess plastic. Think about how it can stick out if you try to tuck it real quick."

That nigga is fulla game! Raynard thought as he hopped out of Mike's car and walked toward the crowd in front of Redford High School. He waved and slapped hands with old classmates until he reached the raised flowerbed encased in concrete called "the circle". He sat on the circle with a bunch of students waiting for the bus to take them to their classes at different vocational schools.

A blue, Ford Escort pulled up. The window eased down and Dirty leaned out. "You got scuds?" he asked, referring to Raynard's dime bags. Before blunts came about, Raynard remembered calling his joints scud missiles, named after the artillery used in the Desert Storm war back then.

Dirty wore a patch over one eye, and usually rode with Rob and T.C.

Raynard sprang upright and went over to serve Dirty.

Five minutes passed before Raynard noticed Roy and Smurf. They walked over and bought a few bags.

"Where y'all goin'?" Raynard asked after noticing the two headed toward the library across the street.

Smurf turned his head. "It's a skip party in Brightmoor. You need to come!"

Raynard declined, remembering how outrageous skip parties were sometimes back then. He just wanted to see Pat. He realized he didn't even know where to go if he went inside the school, so he went to the payphone at the library to call Pat.

"Hello?" Pat exhaled through phone, sounding as if she were still in dreamland.

"Hey! What you doin'?" Raynard asked. His dick was instantly stone just hearing her voice.

"Dang. What's wrong with you?" Pat asked.

"Nothin'. I'm just happy to hear your voice," he said, knowing she sounded pretty much the same as her older self. It was the fact that they were so in love at that time that had his blood scorching.

"I was just with you last night."

"For real?" slipped out in his excitement.

"Oh, you bein' funny?"

"Just messin' with you. I'm startin' to miss you already," he said, wondering what type of magic show he'd been a part of.

"I miss you, too," she said simply.

He hadn't heard that voice speak those words since Tupac was alive. He knew she was sincere. He had no thoughts of sex, or her naked body, but his dick was hard as the chewing gum under the desk in study hall. To make things worse, he was in an era where he wore boxers. Phone booths had already disappeared, so he was standing at a payphone out in the open wearing Guess Jeans with a baggy cut. His bulge was so intense in front; the rear of his jeans was fitting tight around his butt. "Let me come see you."

"Ain't you s'posed to be in school?"

"I was but, they havin' some stupid assembly about the importance of safe sex. I didn't feel like I needed to go 'cause we already do it like we do it, and I don't need to do it to nobody else."

"Awwww," she moaned. So you wanna come pull up in your parkin' spot?"

Damn my shit hard! Raynard thought, feeling like his high school erection was worthy of spitting out semen with enough force to break a window. "Can I come over?"

"You know you can come over anytime, boy. We already talked about that. But, you know I gotta watch Stevie today."

Stevie was Pat's younger brother. He was the same age as Raynard, but after eating paint chips his mental development froze at the age of three. Stevie wore a diaper most of the time and stood five-nine. Eating sweets loosened his bowels almost instantly, and if Stevie had an accident, something more than his diaper would need to be thrown away.

"You know Stevie is my guy!" Raynard lied. He hated when Stevie came around because Stevie always had some kind of outrageous request he needed only Raynard to deliver on. If and when Raynard failed to make things happen for Stevie, Stevie would cry like a spoiled three-year-old. There was no way Raynard could get Pat's buttons unfastened with an oaf like Stevie on deck. On one occasion Raynard promised to bring Stevie a penguin.

"Okay, if you want," Pat told Raynard.

Raynard asked, "So, do you want me to bring the Eighteen Hundred Silver?

"The what?"

"The eighteen—" Raynard caught himself, realizing the Silver edition hadn't been introduced to the market at that time. "Oh, my bad, Hennessy! Right? Hennessy."

"Why you actin' so weird today, baby?"

"It's just a crazy ass dream I had, that's all."

After hanging up, Raynard couldn't see himself wasting time at the bus stop so he began jogging down McNichols in Pat's direction, looking back every few blocks for the iron pimp. Before he knew it, he was at Evergreen. He decided to stop at the bus stop by Chauncey's Records, knowing that if he arrived too tired, he would be filth in bed. He realized he wasn't even tired from the jog—not even breathing hard. He felt wonderful enough to just jog the entire way, but had no intention of taking that much time to get there. *How fuckin' long this bus take anyway?* he thought after two minutes. Knowing he'd just made a few bucks, he decided to flag a taxi.

Every cab passing seemed to be from the Blue Eagle Company, filled with special needs kids.

Being bored and pissed off, he peeked in the window of the record store. Chauncey wasn't open yet and had the blinds pulled down. Raynard could still see through the cracks enough to make out a young woman wearing a "move somethin'" skirt, cleaning and dusting the place while Rocky manned the store. Rocky walked over and sat in his chair behind the counter. The young woman, looking to be in her mid-twenties, had a rag in her hand, polishing the counters. She worked her way over to Rocky who took her in his embrace, placing a hand on her magnificently shaped ass as she planted kisses all over his face. He rubbed her rear before sliding the hand beneath her skirt, lifting it. He palmed and squeezed her left cheek as if he were paid to do so while his lips flapped near her ear. Rocky smacked her bottom as she spun on her heels and headed for the back room with him closely behind.

Raynard could only imagine what kind of employee meeting was going on in there, and the thoughts once again had him on bone. By that time, the McNichols was screeching to a halt. He hopped in and paid his fare.

Raynard exited the bus, unzipping his jacket since the May sun was starting to beam. He crossed the busy street to reach the only store he knew he would be able to get the liquor from. As he touched the store's door handle, he could hear the voices inside.

"And hear come this slick bastard," Tricky Rick said.

"What you mean?" Raynard asked, not knowing why Tricky could be sore with him.

"Man, you sold me that tight-ass bag yesterday! We couldn't get but two joints outta it!"

Raynard looked to Greg who was slowly shaking his head. "You stingy as hell," Greg told him.

Raynard stepped close to Tricky and whispered in his ear, "Grab me a pint of Hennessy."

Tricky's eyebrows rose with surprise. "Now you want me to do somethin' for you? Man, you too much. I don't know, bruh. Seem like you do me as bad as you can."

Raynard knew Tricky just wanted more weed. "Man, come on."

"You gon' have to donate a joint for me and puppy nuts! We bought that bag with our last and--"

"Okay," Raynard said, cutting him off. He just wanted the bottle so he could get to Pat. He walked to the back of the store and pinched a joint worth from one of his dime bags and handed it to Tricky along with cash for the liquor. He walked to the counter behind and Tricky and bought a box of Lemonheads. He followed Tricky outside where he received his bag.

Raynard almost came up short as he bolted across the busy street. In the blink of an eye, he was on Pat's porch, jabbing the bell. Just the sounds of Pat's footsteps nearing the door raised Raynard's flag.

The door swung open and Pat stood there in a t-shirt that wouldn't have been long enough to tuck into any pair of pants. She was far sexier than he remembered with her hair pulled back into a ponytail. *Candies* was printed around the band of her full, red panties. Raynard realized she was that deal even before the invention of the thong, standing there with her magnificent hips choked by the cotton material. He couldn't ever remember being that hard as a forty-year-old, and was in a rush to use his youthful boner.

"You gon' just stand there?" she asked, snapping him out of his trance. "Damn! What you got in there?" she asked, noticing his menacing erection.

Raynard dropped the liquor on the table and wrapped his arms around Pat. She embraced him as his hands dropped down past her shirt to the dizzying softness of her ass. He squeezed and rubbed as he thanked The Lord for his blessings.

"Stop. You gon' make me wet like that," she said in a honeyed tone.

Lowering his head, his tongue imposed a sugary tax upon hers.

"Ssssss," came through her teeth with a deep inhale as she gripped his eager love sickle through his jeans. "You know we can't in front of Stevie."

Raynard had forgotten about Stevie who was in the corner playing with army men. "How long is he gon' be here?" he asked.

"My mother went to the casino in Canada with Ms. Ricks, so, you know how that can turn out."

Shit, that can be all damn day! Raynard had travelled the sands of time to get that pussy, and there was no way Stevie was going to hold him up. "Well, what you do when you gotta go to the bathroom? I know you don't take him with you, do you?"

"Boy, stop it. You just horny."

"Naw, it's more than that. You don't understand." Raynard held her hand and looked through her eyes into her soul. "I love you, Pat. I never knew just how much until recently..." He spent a full ten minutes spilling his heart, even tossing in a few lines from the movie "The Notebook" since it wouldn't be out for years.

She grabbed Raynard by the hand, and after snatching a pillow from the sofa, she led him into the bathroom.

"Him gotta potty?" asked Stevie.

"Yes, Stevie, he gotta potty," she said before closing the door.

Raynard dropped his pants to his ankles. His eyes were held captive by the sorcery in her wiggling out of her panties.

After closing the toilet, Pat dropped the pillow on top of the lid. Bending over, she planted the side of her face on the pillow, and placed a hand on the window seal for balance.

Raynard stumbled toward her, taking his time to caress and rub her perfect derrière. He gripped his shaft and began teasing them both by playfully rubbing the head across her slippery opening until he just couldn't take it anymore and infiltrated her love.

He pushed himself in her--just past the head--then pulled back. Thrusting forward again, he went in until her cheeks pressed against his waistline and his balls boinged against her clitoris. The inside of her womb felt golden and his only thought was marriage. He slowly withdrew, looking down at his glistening shaft.

Remembering Stevie, Raynard hoped that guy wouldn't find a jelly bean under the couch leftover from Easter. He knew he had the world spinning in his unlotioned hands, but the clock was ticking, so from the rear, he dogged Pat like a rental car. She sobbed and winced until she brought Raynard to a climax so spectacular he found himself hunched over and on his tippy-toes.

Raynard withdrew his pipe, wondering how she took it all since it looked as if it had been exposed to gamma rays even as it deflated.

With a foot on the toilet, Pat flashed an ivory smile as she swabbed herself with a wet rag. "What I do to deserve that?" she asked.

"Just being beautiful as always," he told her. He knew his time would be soon coming to an end, and he wanted to wake as much as he wanted to be crucified.

Raynard could hear Jenni's hooves bumping their way up the porch steps. He and Jenni couldn't stand one another, and she always found a way to let him know exactly how much.

"Hey, Stevie!" he heard Jenni say as she entered the living room. She sounded cheerful, and if Jenni sounded cheerful after leaving the casino, she had money.

Pat walked up behind Raynard, pushing him into the living room as she walked to greet her mother. She always encouraged Raynard to try to be nice to Jenni, but wound up playing referee whenever the two locked horns.

Stevie pointed in the direction of Raynard. "Him doo-doo!"

Jenni's wide grin instantly froze over as Raynard entered the living room. "You got that right, baby, him doo-doo!" Her words were laced with venom.

"I just came to say 'hello' to you. How are you, Jenni?" Raynard said in his pleasant, Mr. Roger's voice.

Jenni simply twisted her lips and said, "Well, you can at least help Stevie pick up all them damn toys.

"Dang! For real?" Pat asked as Raynard moved over by Stevie.

Raynard smiled while his back was to Pat. He had an arsenal of irritating things planned for Jenni. Things he'd picked up in the future years.

Raynard was on his knees scooping Stevie's platoon of soldiers off the carpet, dumping them in Stevie's backpack as Jenni told Pat of all the excitement in Canada. He knew Stevie was watching carefully and allowed no one to touch his backpack, so Raynard made sure he didn't. But, he did retrieve the box of Lemonheads from his pocket and slid them into the backpack. Stevie saw and began to clap.

Raynard heard Jenni say, "I see them blazin' sevens every time I close my eyes!" as he quickly zipped the backpack.

Stevie opened his mouth and sounded the alarm. Slobber oozed from his mouth as he hollered and pointed at Raynard.

"What the hell you doin' to my son?" Jenni asked.

Raynard stood. "I just zipped his backpack. I thought you asked me to help him?"

"Come on, baby," Jenni told Stevie.

Raynard rejoiced inside as Jenni's foot left the last step. He finally had Pat all to himself. He embraced her tightly, squeezing her ass with both hands. He walked her over to the couch. They kissed deeply as he eased her onto her back, lying on top of her. He was hard like he had done nothing earlier. He slid her panties down past her thighs and off her feet. After slowly easing into her, Raynard stroked while sucking her bottom lip. Their love made a sound like mac and cheese being stirred.

The next thing Raynard knew, he was on his back, reaching in air for his Goddess.

CHAPTER 6

Raynard felt Pat's huge weight as her left arm lay across his stomach and she rested down near his waist. The mac and cheese symphony was now a crescendo of sucking and slurping sounds as an obese Pat orally worked out Raynard's concrete pleasure giver.

Pat hadn't lost her touch when it came to giving head, and Raynard knew he had to shit Tiffany Cufflinks in order to get her to do it nowadays. He felt irritable and cranky, but still tried to enjoy the suck job even though he hated her fat ass touching him. The morning sunbeams in his eyes weren't helping any. He really wanted to go and get more dope to shake the bullshit feeling he had, but he knew there was no way to stop Pat now; she already had the taste of dick in her mouth. Besides, he knew she would never allow him to waste his wonderfully petrified soul roll by coming in her mouth; he would have to bury it in her grossness if he wanted to bust.

Raynard's face twisted in disgust as Pat bobbed for a minute, then right before he neared a climax; she took it out of her mouth and began licking the sides. He wished he was bigger so he could've just shoved her onto the floor, but over the years his coke habit sponged away his appetite and kept him scrawny. As he wondered just how long she'd been violating him, he decided to reach for the only sensible angle to give them both what they wanted.

"Get up," he told her.

"Uhn-uh," she said between slurps.

"Man, get up so I can beat that pussy up!" he said, dangling her desires in the direction he wanted her to move.

Pat turned and looked back at him. Her face was wet from her nostrils to her chin. A light beam squeezed through the blinds and ignited blinding twinkles in a cable of spittle that stretched from her bottom lip to his penile head.

Raynard begin to get up as Pat moved to her knees and elbows in the doggy-style position. He got behind her and immediately frowned; wishing she had been a little more surgical when it came to wiping her ass, but he still had a throbbing erection to deal with. Pulling apart her bovine cheeks, he pushed himself in. He gripped her between two of her rib rolls and went to work. He had to throw his head back for a minute and sniff hard, feeling like something was about to run out of his nose and onto Pat's butt.

"Oh, shit! Shit!" she hollered as he angrily mule-dicked her. "Oww, it's too deep!" he heard her say as he released inside her.

As she laid shaking and rubbing her legs together, Raynard grabbed his cell phone and headed for the restroom. He closed the door and pressed Ike's number into the phone's keypad.

No answer. He hawked up a glob of phlegm and spat it into the toilet.

This shit ain't gon' work, he thought as he watched the loogie—loaded with crimson streaks and bubbles—whirl around until it was out of sight. He needed more dope and knew he didn't have any money. He was a week away from getting another SSI check, and had heard nothing from the streets on making a quick dollar. He knew Pat had plenty of money tucked away, but he would need to tie on his boxing gloves to ask her.

I gotta get me a normal bitch! ...At least somebody who like me. Man, wait 'til I get me a couple dollars..., he thought as he lathered his face towel with soap in preparation for his quick birdbath in the sink before hitting the streets.

"Where you goin'" Pat asked as Raynard speed-dressed.

"Just goin' to see if I can make a couple dollars."

"Doin' what?"

"Whatever I can to make some money. You got some you wanna share with me?"

"Huh? You say you wanna eat my what?"

"Yeah, right! You know I didn't say that."

"But for real, why don't you ever do it for me like you used to?" Pat sincerely asked.

"Do what?" Raynard knew well what she was getting at. He sniffed.

"Eat my pussy. You need to quick playin' like you don't know what's up."

"It's not good to do on a empty stomach." He tried his damndest to hold back his smile.

"Yup. That's alright, baby! You just gone out there and get yo' hands dirty in them streets. I keep me some money. I might buy you a blow sometime if you treated me better. But, that's ok."

"Why don't you just throw me a few bucks, then I'll be in a better mood. No tellin' what can happen then."

"I'm straight. I can just wait til' you wake up hard again. But, hey, you know what its gon' take if you want some money from me!"

"So you trickin' wit me now?"

"Naw, 'cause you ain't participatin'."

Raynard knew Pat had money. He had no idea as to how much. They lived rent-free since it was Johnny Cash's house and he used it from time to time to stash drugs and other hot things he didn't want under his own roof. Raynard and Pat split the cost of the utilities, and both received food stamps. The remainder of his cash was usually inhaled, but Pat was a cheapskate and guzzled inexpensive booze. After the utilities and her liquor bill, Pat was able to stack the majority. When she went on the shopping trips with Jenni, Pat would cry broke so

Jenni would treat and, over drinks, do her best at trying to hypnotize Pat into leaving Raynard.

Raynard hadn't put his tongue to Pat since the last Christmas season, hoping she would supersize whatever it was he had coming. He couldn't see himself doing a nosedive in the next few months when the holidays returned—gift or no gift.

He knew he had screwed up in life. Mike Mo's words echoed in his head. His experiences seemed so real, he figured he'd found a way to go back and do it all again, knowing what he currently knew. He just wished he could some way change things in the past so that the changes would affect his current and future status. The blows he was taking didn't allow him much time on each trip, but at least he got to spend time and make love with a fine woman who loved and wanted him. With his current mind, and Pat's back in the day package, he felt he could move mountains. Thoughts of Pat's silver smile had Raynard's dick stretching his undies.

Raynard reached for the front door then realized, *she is bein' way too quiet in there.* He headed for the bedroom where Pat would without a doubt be disappearing cupcakes while watching reality soaps. She had the door closed.

He gripped the doorknob and carefully pulled the door to him so it wouldn't pop open as he twisted the knob. Inching it open, he placed his eyeball in the crack. Pat was standing, wearing only a bra with her back to the door. He chuckled to himself thinking of the old Hustler Comic where the fat lady was looking for her husband, only to realize he was trapped in her buns.

Pat turned toward the mirror, stuffing a wad of bills she'd been counting into her bosom.

Money! he saw. Raynard quickly moved through the doorway. "What you in here doin'?"

Startled, Pat jumped, then placed her hand on her hip. "You need to stop snoopin' around!"

Motivated by her bankroll, Raynard tried to take charge, grabbing her arm in an attempt to move her to the bed.

Pat had no idea what was going on. She pulled away. "What you doin'? Why you grabbin' all on me?"

He knew he couldn't just take it if he wanted to, so without uttering a word, Raynard undid his belt and top button, allowing his pants to fall freely. He pulled his semi-hard joint from his boxers and tried again. He pushed Pat easily onto the bed. The springs complained as she sank into the mattress.

Still with his pants around his ankles, Raynard pulled his shirt over his head and climbed between Pat's parting legs. Her eyeballs disappeared underneath their lids as he poked into her murky nest and commenced to doing the horizontal hula. He really tried his best at getting her off again, knowing he had a better chance of getting blow-fare while his dick was in her. He began to think of how okay things could be between the two of them if their relationship wasn't in shambles and Pat wasn't so mean all the time.

In the push up position, Raynard humped until sweat beads erupted from his forehead. He noticed the money captive in her bra and humped harder, trying to bounce her breasts and free it. Not only did the cash fly out, but so did her huge tits, rippling like a rhythm meter as he pumped his bony ass.

"Damn! What's all that?" Raynard asked.

"My money."

"Why you got it in there like that?"

"'Cause I was about to go to the store and get me somethin' to drink."

"'Bout to get yo' buzz on!" He watched her lids again veil her eyes as he bottomed her out, completely spending himself inside her. "Can I get my buzz on, too?" he asked as she clenched her vaginal muscles, wringing the last bit of man juice out of his deflating organ.

"I guess you deserve a blow today, big daddy!" Her words brought warmth to Raynard and eased his stress.

He laid his head down next to hers and began to doze, content for the moment since at least he had his blow money. He didn't find her exciting to look at anymore, but definitely found her comfortable to lie on.

* * *

Raynard headed for the store on McNichols. He was pissed. He woke to find Pat had put the shit on him. She was gone and no cash was on the bed. He dressed again, and hurried to the front door to find her camped out on the couch. She had her plastic cup and was smiling.

"What up? You got them couple dollars for me?" He was starting to get irritated by the joking smirk she wore.

Pat aimed a loud belch Raynard's way. It smelled like Vienna Sausages.

"Man, quit playin'." He took a deep breath. He wanted to cuss her out sooo bad.

"We already talked about what you gotta do for me to give you some money."

"Pat, come on, baby. You said I deserve a blow."

"See, if it was just that you needed money that would be different. But, I don't want you doin' blows!"

"Well, why you gotta drink?"

Pat cheesed, then shot another belch his way.

Raynard walked in the store to see Tricky Rick in the rear by the pop coolers, looking as if he were trying to sell some young damsel a dream. Tricky was funky fresh with razor creases in his True Religion getup. After hearing the damsel say, "Damn, you clean. Let me touch you," Raynard quickly grabbed a few canned soups and other groceries while Tricky was occupied, because Rick would go deep into his bag of jokes when he noticed Raynard busting food stamps at the counter.

Raynard sniffed.

From the rear of the store, Tricky Rick sniffed.

Raynard's head twisted at the sniff. He saw Tricky on the other side of the potato chip rack, peeking through with a sinful grin. Making a mental note to try and hold his sniffs until he got outside, Raynard turned and talked with the guy behind the counter for a moment. "So, where's Fish Head?" he asked.

"Who? You mean, Greg?" asked the clerk. "He's asleep in back."

Raynard could only imagine the divine happiness Greg was smiling to back there. *Damn, I gotta get me some get-highs!* Without even thinking, Raynard sniffed twice.

Tricky Rick sniffed twice, making the damsel explode in high-pitched laughter. The damsel headed for the door, and Tricky stepped toward Raynard.

As he headed for the door, Rick blocked his exit. "I got them good blows."

"Didn't we just go through this the other day?"

"I'm just lookin' out. I know your mans got raided this mornin'." Tricky made large, teasing eyes.

Aw, shit! Raynard got a sick feeling in his gut.

"Here," Tricky said as he pressed a small, folded piece of a lottery printout into Raynard's hand. "Have one on me."

Raynard looked down at his hand, then reached to give the blow back. Tricky's hands were already in his pockets. Raynard said, "Ok, but, I keep tellin' you, I don't fuck with 'em. I'll find somebody to give it to."

"Shit, I don't care," Tricky said. "Keep on fuckin' with that bullshit if you want. I know you see it's burnin' out your mucosa."

Raynard had an attitude about the way he was being cut into, but still had to ask, "My what?"

"Your mucus membranes, nasal cavity--all that! That's why you sniffin' all the time."

Tricky Rick's ball-breaking had Raynard mad enough to want to fight. "Yeah, ok." He started out the door.

"Did you ever see puppy nuts with the sniffles?"

"Naw, but I seen his ass sleep in public, lookin' crazy! I ain't tryin' to fuck with nothin' I'm gon' be hooked on and shit!"

Tricky peeked from under his True Religion fisherman hat. "Oh, really," he said with a know-it-all look that extinguished the debate.

Feeling checkmated humility, Raynard started toward his car. He heard the store's door open.

"What you gon' be doin' while I'm stretchin' out that bad bitch I just met, huh? Sniffin' the beat to The Star Spangled Banner?"

I wonder why the fuck his ho-ass keep pressin' me to do that bullshit? he thought, doubting Tricky could have seen him as having the potential to be the next puppy nuts.

Raynard made his way to the alley where he'd copped the day before and found only crucifying depression. It was deserted except for Pitbull, who was trying to hack his way through the wall with a screwdriver. Raynard sniffed and kept on through the alley.

As he came out onto Freeland and turned right facing Fenkell, he peeked into the rearview mirror and saw headlamps beaming a Morse coded message. *Blows, blows, come get your blows!* was Raynard's interpretation of the message. He juked the gear shifter into reverse, and whirred back until he reached a small, red compact. No hug could've compared to the smiles exchanged as Raynard's passenger door neared Ike's.

Raynard parked, then hopped from his car into Ike's. "Why you down here?" asked Raynard, playing it off like he never heard of the raid.

"They hit us. Narcs came early and stomped our security, then came on in there."

"They stomped him out?" Raynard asked, nearly busting a nut to the splendid news.

"Yeah, he a soldier, but they dogged him. Matter of fact, they went hard on everybody in there. I wasn't even up yet."

"What about Lenard?" Raynard hoped he at least got his finger jammed for acting like he didn't know him when he stood in line.

"Man, I doubt if that nigga eye could fit in this car."

Cool! "So, why you sittin' right here?"

"Tryin' to catch some of our customers."

"Damn! Look like you officially a street nigga! Spot get hit and you back on the block in a matter of hours, servin' custos." He wanted to hype Ike up and make him feel good as possible, knowing he didn't have a slug to spend.

"Yeah, but, what's up with you?"

"Shit, I ain't want nothin'—just ridin' through the 'hood," he lied.

"Well, it's hot around here, man. I wouldn't advise you to be in the 'hood today. You better get outta here 'cause I'm dirty as hell," Ike stated while looking in the rear-view as if he expected the boys to show any minute.

Raynard felt like Ike was pushing him out of the car. He wanted a blow bad as hell. He almost bitched out and started begging, but Ike was his man, and he couldn't let Ike see him fiendin' like that...even if Ike was on the puppy nut tip, doing heroin.

He slowly got out and. "Alright, man. Hit me up." He sniffed, then walked back to his car.

Raynard decided to ride back through the alley to see how Pitbull was coming along.

"I'm tellin' you, they got somethin' like a time machine in there!" Pitbull told two plain clothes officers who were shaking him down.

Raynard continued on through, not wanting any smoke from the officers.

He cruised, trying to find a way to come up on a blow. He was missing his baby. The next thing he knew, a green Caddy was riding his ass. *I hate when people do that shit!* he thought, pulling over to allow them room to pass.

The Caddy pulled close to him, rolling down the passenger window. It was the strawberry Cappy was checking out the other night.

"Hi," she began. "Did I see you the other night?"

"Yea. I remember you." It was clear that she was proceeding with caution. He could tell she needed help with something. She spoke proper like she was from suburbia. His street senses were tingling. A blow was on the horizon! He needed to make sure she knew he was cool and connected. "Yea that was the day we was servin' the good stuff a couple blocks over in the alley."

"Excuse me? Did you say you were working there? I thought I saw you in line."

"Yea, yea. I'm part of security. That day I was just playin' it off like I was a custo; kinda like the undercover security in Macy's. Sometimes thangs get disorderly."

"Ok. Smart! Yea, I was looking for you guys. I rode through the alley and didn't see anyone."

"Yea, we had to change the operation up. What you tryin' to do?"

"Well, first I need to know if it's going to be the same stuff."

"Yeah, we got them same ones. Been hangin' out in the past, huh?"

"Yes! It was great! How does that work? What do you guys put in it?"

"Secret recipe," he said. Ready to find an angle on a blow for himself, he continued with, "So, how much you tryin' to spend?" He leaned over the passenger seat and acted like he was checking his phone to sneak in a sniff he hoped she wouldn't hear before his nose began to run.

"Since you said they're the same ones I'll take five."

Yes! Raynard knew he could get a blow for a five-piece sale. "Gimme the money."

"Where's the powder?"

"I gotta run around the corner and get it." Raynard slowed as he spoke, realizing how he sounded to himself.

"Oh, no! I'm not going for that one! If you really work for them, you exchange with me at the same time."

"Ok, ok. See, I would let you come with me, but that's how we got knocked at the other spot. We can't let everybody know where we at." He knew he would be better off if she didn't see Ike. "Wait right here. I'll go get it and come back."

The strawberry looked around at her surroundings, where she would be waiting. "No, that's ok."

Raynard could tell she was scared to sit and wait. He felt his chance to get high diminishing. "Ok, ok. Just wait at the gas station on Strathmoor then. You should be safe there for sure. It's always people in and out."

"Well, how long are you going to be? I'm only going to wait ten minutes."

"That's cool. I just need to run around the corner."

Raynard watched the strawberry turn down Fenkell, then he reversed and went back around the block the long way. He didn't even want her knowing the direction he was going in.

Ike was starting to nod as Raynard walked up. He jumped and acted like he had an attitude after Raynard knocked on the window. He popped the locks. "Damn, nigga," he said as Raynard entered the car.

"What, nigga? Ain't you workin'?"

"Oh, you got some money?" he asked, making it known there would be no freebies.

"Hell yeah! A sale for a five-piece!"

"Oooh, that's what I'm talkin' 'bout."

Raynard noticed Cappy's friend, Shorty coming out of the alley. He knew what Shorty was up to the way he looked around, then got to the middle of the sidewalk and looked both ways down the block before starting slowly back towards Fenkell with his head down, obviously racked by some extreme letdown.

"Hurry, give me six blows!" he said as Shorty bent the corner.

"Whoa. You said a five-piece, and you ain't gave me no money yet."

"Man, come on. I got to meet ol' girl right quick, plus I'm gon' serve somebody else."

After serving Shorty and meeting with the strawberry, Raynard came back to Ike.

"I know I get some kinda commission," he told Ike as he handed over the money.

"I got you," Ike said as he gave Raynard a blow.

Raynard left happy as a sissy dancing to disco music. He had a blow, and he even gave the strawberry his number so she could go through him whenever she wanted more blows.

The sun sleepily sank as Raynard made his way home. He hoped Pat was passed out drunk so he could have a peaceful high.

In the kitchen, Raynard microwaved a can of soup, sucked it down, then reached for the remains in a Corona bottle in the fridge. The beer was flat, but it washed down the soup. He wasn't hungry in the first place, but made himself eat something before getting high. He knew the 'cain would take away his appetite, besides, he had hopes of being gone until the next day. He fired up a 'tail that Pat must've left on the sink earlier. Three tokes, then he dropped it down the drain. He cleared his sinuses, hawking it all up as he hovered over the kitchen sink. He dropped the blob in the sink and washed it away with hot water.

"I know yo' triflin' ass ain't spittin' in my sink!" Pat yelled as she swung her purse at his mid-section.

He didn't know what she had in the purse, but it was heavy and hurt him. "You big back bitch! I'm sick of yo' shit."

"Well, you know what the fuck you can do!" She punched him in the back. "And don't be callin' me no bitch!" Pat turned and left out of the front door.

Raynard didn't know where Pat was going, and didn't care. He did hope she would stay. He stripped and did a cannonball into the bed. He smiled and said, "Yes, sir," as he reached for the cd case on the nightstand.

CHAPTER 7

"So, what were you sayin' before about us workin' together to make more money?" Pat asked.

Raynard knew he was in bed, and with Pat, but when? He eased his hand over and touched her leg. She instantly moved her nude, figure-eight shape close to him, raising her leg and laying it on his stomach as she nestled close.

Whew! He was home! "Aw, baby, my fault. I was thinkin' 'bout somethin'. Yes, we can do a lot together. We just gotta communicate and trust each other." He was going to make sure things went perfectly that go-around. He wanted them to make cash and stay in love.

"See, that's why I'm glad I got with you. You're younger, but you take charge and you smart. I know you gonna lead us into success!" She placed her hand on his chest and began slowly moving her leg that was across him up and down over his body. "That shit make me so wet," she purred.

The intoxicating feel of her soft skin and the touch of her pubic bristles as she ground against his leg popped his dick up. It landed on his stomach. He gripped her hair near the back of her head and pulled her close. "I love you!"

Pat planted kisses down Raynard's body until she reached his dick. She gripped the base with her hand and skated her tongue around the tip before enveloping the head in her mouth. He closed his eyes and moaned as she took more in. Her free hand lifted his sack and lightly massaged.

Raynard was almost certain Pat had invented fellatio. It was the only thing that could possibly trump sex with her from the rear. Her eloquent tongue seemed to be stealing the skin off of his penis…and making him like it. "Ahhh," he wailed in a sissified tone. Her seed-swallowing techniques had sent him back flipping through Heaven.

After a trip to the bathroom, she snuggled close under his arm. "You smell good; like soap and some weed. You been smokin'?"

He didn't know how she could possibly have known about the 'tail he had smoked, but at that point he was willing to go along with whatever she said. "Yes," he answered as his forefinger stroked her nipple hard. Heart-softening pillow-talk ensued as the two exchanged sweet nothings. It was clear that in that reality, his destiny was paved with the thrills of marital bliss.

* * *

"Man, what's up with that bullshit?" Raynard asked Ike. He was happy to finally be face to face. He'd held back his anger until he was in the car.

"What you mean?" Ike asked, swallowing hard as he looked at Raynard with guilty eyes.

"You pinched that bag I got yesterday! Man, I put in work for that shit. I ain't ask for no freebie!"

"What was wrong with it?"

"Shit, the high didn't last! Soon as it got good, it was over. Why the fuck you gotta play me like that?"

"Dude, I ain't play you like nothin'. That's how the bags are. Fuck it, I'll throw you one."

Raynard saw that Ike was showing the type of respect that he had as they were growing up when Raynard was bigger; but they made sacrifices to different demons, so Ike hadn't missed the meals Raynard had. Ike was now much bigger, and just like with Pat, Raynard doubted that he could whup Ike in his current skeletal state. He decided to pump his brakes. After sniffing once, he said, "Well, shit, man. I ain't trippin'. I ain't have no money, then the blow I did get didn't do what I needed it to."

"Aw, shit. You know how dope is: the more you do, the more you need."

A nightmarish reality started to manifest in Raynard's head. He was going to start having to find a way to up his snort rations. He already was finding it next to impossible to stay fixed as it was. He hated the thought of having to snatch pocket books, but nothing was going to stop him from seeing his baby.

"Hey, you guys got any of those same plays?" sounded the strawberry's voice through Raynard's cell phone.

Raynard turned and nodded to Ike. He was happy as hell. "Yup. We still on. How many you need?"

"Well, I got a couple friends here with me who tried a blow and they want more. What kind of deal can you give us if we each spend fifty?"

Raynard was the king of the mountain. "So, that's one-fifty you wanna spend?" he said loud so that Ike could start preparing his commission. "Hold up, let me crunch some numbers. I will call you back in three seconds," he told her, wanting to take his time and converse with Ike to make sure he was properly compensated. He turned to Ike. "Look, playa…"

"Chill out. I got you. I'll give you nineteen blows. You whack it up how you want."

Raynard quickly did the math in his head. He raised his phone and hit the call button. "Yeah, I can give you one extra. I know, I know. It's raggedy on my end, too. Ok, look, my main man just OK'd you for two extras, but that's it! We almost out—that's the best I can do right now."

Raynard served the strawberry, then Cappy and his crew. He served Shorty without Cappy, then three more 'fiends before deciding to call it quits. His dick was already hard as he whipped and wheeled through his neighborhood trying to make it home to get right.

As soon as he got ready to turn into his driveway, Raynard noticed Jenni's car sitting there. *Ain't this 'bout a bitch!* He'd found a way to get plenty of get highs, and now, Endora, The Queen of Witches was on deck; which meant Stevie would be there, and he would most certainly be on some bullshit!

Raynard wondered how Stevie's little crystal ball was coming along. Raynard got the idea after seeing Stevie mesmerized by The Wizard of Oz. He filled a balloon with collard greens and told Stevie he would be able to see in it like the witch had done with her crystal ball. Knowing that Stevie would let no one get close to his bag, Raynard dropped it in there. He knew that the greens would soon sour and begin to smell like a cadaver until one of Stevie's toy soldiers could get around to popping the balloon with a bayonet.

Raynard knew that if Jenni wasn't parked in the driveway, he could at least go in there and do his dope in peace. *Fuck them punk bitches!* he thought as he stabbed off to find a place to get high.

This shit is almost as bad as not even havin' dope! he thought, knowing he should've been somewhere high as eagle pussy, back in the early nineties with Pat riding his ding-a-ling. He pulled to the store where Tricky Rick seemed to live. He backed into a space in the lot, and looked around. He felt like he was safe where he was since he had Tricky Rick and Greg inside the store to watch his back, plus he was in the 'hood where everyone knew him and it was daytime.

Raynard grabbed a blow off of the passenger seat and found a cd case to put it on. He remembered how he felt the night before about the high not lasting, so he went ahead and dropped half of another one on the case. It didn't look like much more dope than before, so he put the rest of the second blow on the case and did it all.

* * *

Raynard woke breathing hard. He'd had the best time yet! He was in dreamland for what seemed like three days. He and Pat had already begun their financial endeavors. After a sexual triathlon, the two were on their way to New York to cop a trunk load of knock-off purses with fifteen-hundred of Pat's dollars. They planned to sell them around the city.

He reached for another blow, but discovered they were all gone. The passenger door was wide open and the cool night air was starting to add to his irritation. His mouth went dry as he looked around and tried to figure things out. *Tricky Rick did this shit!*

"Hey, man, you been in my car?" Raynard asked in an aggressive tone.

"What? I thought *you* was in yo' car?" Tricky answered, his words dripping with sarcasm.

Raynard was just about ready to scrap when Greg walked over and said, "Li'l Terry was out there a li'l while ago with them young niggas. If it's somethin' missin', he probly got it."

Awwww shit! Raynard knew if Little Terry and company had been around, he would never see his blows again. Terry and crew had the reputation of land pirates. They stole and robbed every chance they got. Fish Head Greg once joked that they even stole the pieces off of Michael Jackson's nose.

Knowing he had Pat's warm rolls waiting for him at home, he decided to ride down Freeland to see if he could work up on more dope.

Raynard got a sick feeling in his gut as he approached a crowd of people standing out on

Freeland. He parked and quickly hopped out. He noticed Mel, so he went to stand by him.

"Sorry to hear about your dog," Mel began.

Raynard looked over and saw yellow tape marking a perimeter around Ike's car. Raynard was frozen with shock.

"Damn, I hope the police don't find no dope on him," Raynard said, hoping he could've somehow had the chance to shake down the car before the cops arrived.

"Shit, I wouldn't worry about that. That nigga, Li'l Terry was the one who found him, so you know if it was anything of value, he got it!"

"What the fuck! So, that nigga killed my mans?" Raynard questioned like he was a badass, ready to kick butt.

"Oh, naw! They say it look like Ike got a hold of some bad dope. Terry just happened along and probly scavenged some shit."

That was it. Raynard was fucked in the game. With Ike over with, and Lenard scared out of the 'hood by pugilistic narcs, Raynard had no chance of getting his high on. He didn't even want to stand around and drink and mourn with the rest of the 'hood.

Raynard felt like he was just sentenced to life in some underground supermax facility and was doomed to never see or hold his woman again. He felt like doing anything; robbery, murder, anything! But even with a gazillion dollars he wouldn't be able to cop what he wanted. The recipe was lost!

CHAPTER 8

It was almost ironic as Raynard realized that he was barely able to cope with the reality that he was trapped in the real world. The only way he could possibly think of to maybe get back to the past would be through Tricky Rick. He had once said something about possessing some of the magical cut, but getting it would be indeed tricky since the old school player had plans of transforming him into the next puppy nuts.

The only thing that kept Raynard from doing a jackknife off The Belle Isle Bridge was the fact that his SSI check would be ready for him that day. As he waited, he flashed back to the night before.

He came home and Pat was posted on the couch as usual, getting to the bottom of her drink.

"What the hell wrong with you?" she asked.

"What I do now?" he asked in a can't-win-for-losing voice.

"You had yo' dopefiend ass at the store noddin' off like that man, Fish Eyes Greg! They been sayin' you gotta be doin' heroin if you noddin' off. I thought it was just crack."

This dumb bitch!

"Now, Sherri and everybody callin' and shit, crackin' all kinda jokes! I'm sicka yo' dopefiend ass."

With no blows to look forward to in his times of need and mourning, he allowed his facial frown to reflect his mood. "Fuck you and them bitches. I'm sicka yo' shit, fat bitch!"

As Pat stood, Raynard began walking toward the bathroom. He could see she was ready to knuckle up and knew he would be trapped, so instead of the bathroom, he opted to go through the kitchen so he could go through the dining room and back to the front door if he had to.

Raynard stood in the kitchen waiting for Pat to give chase, but she walked into the bathroom without a word.

The night seemed the longest and Raynard knew he wasn't getting any sleep. From the infomercials on every channel, he could tell it was at least three a.m. As he went into the bathroom, he noticed Pat still asleep on the couch. *Hell yeah!* he thought, knowing he didn't have the tolerance for her sexual advances.

He pissed and luckily found a moderate-sized cocktail Pat had left on the window seal. It more than likely had been smoked as she took a dump. He fired it up, and as he sucked in his sixth toke, Pat's fist landed in his back, causing a base-filled echo.

I'm gon' get that bitch! he thought as he turned and tried to keep her from seeing his eyes fill with water.

The mail lady's footsteps on the porch were like a musical masterpiece, and Raynard jumped up like he had a lit firecracker in his ass. He grabbed the mail from the box, then ran out into the sunshine.

Every month Raynard cashed his check at the liquor store where Greg and Tricky hung out. He kept a good relationship with the owner so that he could keep a tab. Once he cashed his check and paid his bill, Tricky Rick was right there, waiting.

"Uh, oh!" Greg began. "That boy got a bankroll today."

"Yeah," Tricky said. "Come holla at me, dog."

Raynard stepped to the rear of the store by the soda coolers. "What's the word?"

"Sorry to hear about yo' homeboy. That was some fucked up shit. He had it goin' on, too."

"Raynard dropped his head for a moment. "Yea, thanks."

"Let me know if you need anything. I ain't gon' even worry you about my blows or nothin'. I see you goin' through some rough stuff right now…"

Raynard knew Tricky wasn't trying to sell him blows because if they were needed everyone would have to go to him to get down. He sniffed to get up his courage. "Well, come to think of it, I could use some of that cut you was tellin' me about."

"What, you tryin' to put a bag together?" Tricky asked, obviously checking for potential competition.

"Naw. Just for me. A li'l somethin'."

"Mmmm, let me think." Tricky looked for the answers on the ceiling. How much you got to spend on somethin' like that?" he asked.

Raynard already knew he would have to grab his ankles, but was prepared for the financial rape in order to get back to his baby. "Let me take care of these couple bills and come back. It should at least be a couple hundred."

"Aw, shit, man. I thought you was ready!" He turned to Greg. "This dude up in here actin' like he ready to get down."

"He just perpetratin'," Greg co-signed.

Tricky's face reflected disgust. "Man, holla at me when you ready! I ain't got time for games."

Just knowing that he would be able to cop had Raynard hyped. He turned on the radio and sang along with every song that was played until he got home. He ran in the house, left his half of the bills on the kitchen table, then stashed fifty for bad weather. He folded the rest of his bankroll and headed for the liquor store.

Geeked as hell, he parked and hopped out of the car, prancing his way into the store. He heard the driver door of the car next to his open, then heard his passenger door open. He twisted his head around. *Awww, shit!* He'd paid no attention to his surroundings and now Terry was in his ride. He ran back. "Aye! What the fuck you doin'?"

Terry didn't flinch. He continued rummaging through the glove compartment. Once Raynard was close enough, Terry pointed a small handgun at him. "Where that shit at?"

"What shit?" He sniffed.

"Oh, you gon' play with me? Nigga somebody stole my whole SSI check and I heard you had somethin' to do with it!" Terry said, trying to justify the shakedown.

"Man, I ain't do shit! Anyway, you got me the other day for my blows!"

"Oh, so they *was* your blows? Yea, I knew you was out here gettin' money. I ain't do it, but I heard about it." Terry bared his fangs. "Now, where the fuck is my money, nigga? You gon' give me my shit…some blows or somethin'!"

Raynard looked Terry in the eyes and knew he would bust a cap in broad daylight. Terry's eyes were huge and whirling around in his skull like he had done a jaw full of ecstasy so Raynard knew he didn't have much time to think. "Ok, look, man…I don't know what's up with your money, but I only got a few dollars. Here." Raynard reached in his pocket and tried to slip a couple of bills off of his bankroll.

"Nigga, I see you pinchin' off that knot! You better run all that shit!"

By the time the store owner made his way outside, Terry was screeching away through the alley behind the store. "Somebody gonna kill his ass," said the storeowner.

Raynard didn't even know why he was going in the store behind the owner; he didn't have anything in his pockets.

"Man, that nigga, Li'l Terry got me outside!" he told Tricky Rick and Greg.

Greg lifted his chin off his chest. "What? Is he still out there?"

Tricky Rick stood unfazed, focusing his attention on whatever he was digging from under his fingernails with a toothpick. "I keep tellin' y'all niggas; watch what the fuck goin' on around you! I don't know how you let *that* nigga get up on you like that."

Raynard couldn't remember how either. "Man, I need that cut, too."

"I'll give you a eighth of it for one twenty-five."

"Damn, that nigga fucked me up. I only got like, fifty left, dog."

"Shiiit, I can do nothin' for that but five blows." Tricky looked up and paused. "I might even be able to throw you six."

"Man, I can't do nothin' with that," Raynard said while Tricky got back to his nail cleaning.

Tricky's shoulder gave Raynard a bad case of freezer burn and sent him on his way home.

Raynard once again felt like all hope was lost. Terry had shattered his dreams. He had no idea how he was going to make it until his next SSI check.

"Hey," Pat began. "Give me a couple dollars to pay the paperboy. I ain't got no change."

"I ain't even got it right now." Raynard said in a low tone.

"Are you serious? You just got your check!" Pat went silent after telling the paperboy to come back later.

Raynard felt useless as pussy to the Pope. He knew he had a fifty tucked away, but had no desire to cop a regular blow—no matter how potent. He wanted to get back to his baby. He needed her like he needed his small intestine.

He stopped by the bathroom to take a leak and found, for some reason Pat had neglected to flush the toilet. It smelled like she'd left behind something that died three seasons ago. Raynard felt too down to even fuss or talk about her. Figuring she had forgotten while rushing out to catch the front door, he simply flushed and did his business. He hated that the picture of what was in that toilet had been chiseled into his head.

Even though it was too early for Pat to even be drunk yet, he went and got in bed. It only made sense for a flock of buzzards to circle overhead as depression pinned him to the mattress and began slowly sucking the life out of him.

He looked to the cd case he'd used so many times to snort dope off of and laid his head back down. It was cleaner than the day he bought it.

The free blow from Tricky Rick, he remembered, reasoning that the dope should've fallen off and become weak by then. His hopes were that the cut was still filled with magic.

He dug the blow out of his jacket pocket, then sat on the bed. He opened the folded piece of lottery ticket and sat there looking at it for a couple of minutes. The powder was beige and looked to be about the same amount he received when he bought coke. He looked over to the cd case. *Fuck it!* he decided, and tossed the paper and all into his mouth.

He leaned back on his fists. A wonderful wave of euphoria washed though Raynard's body. He looked to the closed door and noticed Pat peeking through a crack in it. He didn't give a damn; he was feeling things that could only be rivaled by busting a nut.

Realizing she'd been made, Pat opened the door. "You need to get checked out," she began,

Bitch, you just hate to see me happy! He knew when he saw her eyeball in the crack that she would find a way to ruin his moment of precious serenity.

"I knew you was on dope and shit, but yo' ass is crazy!"

Raynard immediately felt woozy. Before he could lift his back pockets off of the mattress, he heaved and puked chunks. He heard Pat say,"Uuugh! Damn that shit stank!" before he fell back and flew the friendly skies.

CHAPTER 9

Raynard woke after what seemed like a week on the other side with the younger version of Pat. He looked down to see Pat's back rolls as she laid a little lower on the bed. He could feel her holding his limp organ.

"See, that wasn't the same stuff! I'm up here thinkin' you gon' wake up hard again…yo' shit like jelly! You fuckin' up! Well, you definitely know what you gon' have to do if you run outta money and wanna get high. Mamas gon' be waitin'."

I'd rather suck a sour dish rag before I put my mouth on yo' fat ass!

*　　　*　　　*

Raynard walked out of the bathroom, looking over at the couch to make sure Pat was asleep. He crept into the kitchen and took her purse off of the table, then with cat burgling stealth, he tip-toed back into the bathroom. He turned the water on in the sink to cover any noise he might make, and proceeded to ramble. He took out the bill folder and flicked through some of the pictures. He found a shot of the two of them from the past, when times were good. He was mesmerized by the way she clung to him so possessively. It was just like in the dream state when he got high. He slipped the photo out and put it in his back pocket. He went to the section where she kept her cash. He saw what looked to be a few hundred, so he took a twenty.

I deserve this shit, he told himself, thinking of the way she'd been doing him lately. He folded quickly under the weight of the monkey on his back, and had been keeping his face in Pat's nether regions to stay fixed since he couldn't get hard for her off the "diesel".

Ever since he popped the first blow into his mouth, he'd been dangling from Tricky Rick's heroin noose. Ninety days later, Raynard ran Rick's errands with the jiffyness. He'd been getting what seemed like two weeks away with his baby every time he got high. Sometimes Tricky Rick would let him move a bundle or two if he felt sorry enough for him.

He was on edge so bad he was stealing Pat's cash. He had just come out of a high where things went so well, he had proposed to his boo. He wanted to get back there bad as hell.

Things were all bad when it came to him eating Pat. She would throw him five bucks for head, unless he made her cum. Making her cum was trickier than French kissing a Venus flytrap, because Pat had a bad habit of clenching up when he got her off. Until she stopped shaking, his neck would be in the scissors, cutting off his air and circulation to his head. He just didn't feel like risking his life for ten dollars at that time unless he absolutely had to.

Having enough to get high then and still one to wake up on, he went to take the purse back to the kitchen. He crept in, gently dropped the purse, and turned. Pat came from behind the wall in the dining room.

"You raidin' my purse now?" She had her hand on her hip.

Damn, I know I'm gon' have to scrap with this drunk bitch! He watched Pat go through her belongings.

"Aw, hell naw! I got all kinda shit missin'!"

As she neared him, his heart threw a tantrum. She lunged forward with her arms outstretched, obviously not knowing he had a bit of rabbit in him. Raynard turned and slipped through her clutches like a buttered eel. He went back through the living room, and out the front door. He stopped when he reached the grass, because he knew she wouldn't give chase past the porch since the time she fell down the stairs.

At the store, Raynard stepped in and headed straight for Tricky Rick.

"There he go," said Tricky. He had on a cash colored linen outfit with booger-green gators on his feet.

"I like that," Raynard said. "Yeah, me and my girl was thinkin' 'bout startin' a clothin' line and droppin' some camouflage linen outfits."

Tricky Rick nonchalantly said, "Ooo, I can't wait to suit up in some of that shit," while he cleaned his fingernails with a straightened paperclip.

"Let me get two," Raynard said, cutting the small talk. He tucked his blows in his pocket, then asked, "Hey, can I help you move a bundle or two tomorrow?"

"I gotta see. I been gettin' a few complaints about you."

Raynard knew it was a good chance Rick would put him on. Rick always seemed to blame him for something to keep his balls in a vice. "I'll hit you up tomorrow." Raynard spun on his heels and left.

Knowing things would be funky if he went back home, Raynard tried to think of a place he could go to get high in peace.

He wheeled through the 'hood, thinking of where he could go. His previous encounter with Terry had him thinking more about safety than he did before; especially doing heroin which was a downer and a powerful sedative.

He stopped to see Paris on the corner of Mark Twain and Florence. Paris was cool and sometimes had powder cocaine to sell. Raynard knew him for years and knew he had a good chance of getting high in the basement where Paris and the rest of his buddies would be playing video games. Paris had a dime piece for a live-in. Her name was Lovey, and she shook her ass at The Sting, on Michigan Avenue.

"Hey, man, what y'all got up?" Raynard asked Paris.

"Nothin'. We just down here chillin', playin' the game. What up with you?"

"Aw, man. I fell out with Pat dumb ass."

"Damn, sorry to hear that. Well, you can chill down there with us, then when everybody leave, just crash on the couch down there. Chill for a couple days 'til y'all get it together."

That was all Raynard needed to hear. He had a few days of peace to look forward to. Raynard shuffled past Paris and company as they jabbed buttons on the game controllers. He settled on the couch in the rear of the basement. He especially liked the positioning of the coach since it was in a dark shadowed section of the basement and no one would be paying him much attention.

Leaning to the side, he snorted a blow, not worried about being heard since the video game was being played through the house speakers, and sounded as if they were courtside at The Palace. He sat back in his seat and noticed Paris coming his way.

"Hey, man. Can Lovey use your car to go to work? She get off at like, two, but I didn't think you was goin' anywhere… She'll probly throw you somethin' when she get back—she get it in on Thursdays!"

'Nuff said! He tossed Paris the keys without uttering a word. It was on. The powerful opiate pulled the shades down over the windows to Raynard's soul. He was now one with the poppy.

* * *

"Hold up, I thought you said I could chill a couple days?" Raynard asked Paris, after waking to a letdown.

"I know, man. It ain't me."

"Damn. Alright." After dealing with Pat he could kind of understand. After all, Paris was undoubtedly hooked by Lovey, who was rumored to have had the best pussy on the west side.

As Raynard reached the front door, he asked Lovey, "Where the keys?"

"They in the car," she answered while stepping behind Paris.

In the car? Raynard walked out, followed by Paris. His car was parked on the side of the house with front end damage consistent with being wrapped around a pole or hydrant. "What the fuck?" he shouted.

"I know, man. Told her you was gon' trip. We gon' tighten' you up. Don't even worry 'bout it."

Lovey peeked around Paris. "I know you mad, but somebody jumped out in front of me…"

"My car is totaled! No wonder you want me to leave."

"Naw, naw, it ain't like that," she began. "You be jerkin' around and smilin' and stuff in your sleep. You gon' scare the kids!"

Raynard walked a half block, then realized he didn't even get a buck for letting her use the car. He doubled back. He knocked, then pounded the door. No answer after five minutes, so he started his three-block trek home. He didn't want to go, but he still had another blow. The one he'd just woke from gave him a taste of the married life, and just how splendid lovemaking could be after working with his woman to stack twenty thousand in ten days.

He had nothing of the sort taking place in his current reality. He was *walking* home for the first time in years. He knew when he got there Pat would be ready to slip on a pair of skis before she put her foot in his ass. Raynard could only equate his long, slow walk home to the times when he had a bad report card. He tried to look to the brighter side; that maybe hundreds were killed by drunk drivers in the time it took for him to make it home. Too bad he couldn't think of any way to package that argument and sell it to Pat.

Yes! he thought at the sight of Jenni's car in the driveway. *I know my nigga Stevie got my back!*

Raynard remembered he'd left his keys in the car and couldn't get in. He dialed Pat's number. "Heeeey!" he faked.

"What the hell you want?" she asked in an almost playful way. "Mama in the bathroom, and I'm cleaning Stevie. I'll be down in a minute. Here, talk to Stevie."

Raynard tried to communicate with Stevie over the phone, but couldn't make out anything being said except, "Two bananas."

Pat opened the door, and Raynard expected to be tackled as soon as he walked in, but she acted as if nothing happed.

He quickly went to the bedroom. He went into his pocket for his last blow. *What the fuck?* It was gone.

Raynard sat with his mouth open for about five minutes trying to think whether he dropped it in the car, Paris's basement, or on the way home. *Shit!* He was trapped with no wheels and no blows. He knew Pat was going to tap dance on his skull as soon as her family left. He decided to go to the fridge while company was still in the house.

Pat and Jenni sat in front of the television, laughing at something dumb. Stevie sat in the kitchen, playing with something in the middle of the floor.

Stevie turned and gave Raynard a warm smile. "Got my nanas, Ray Ray?"

Damn. Is that what he was askin'me? Who the fuck need two bananas anyway? Raynard shook his head.

Stevie must've been eating a cracker or had chips in his mouth, because when he opened up to sound the alarm, bits of food used slobber cables to repel from his bottom lip onto his shirt.

At the sound of Stevie's crying, the boom of Pat's footsteps quickly came near. "What the hell you in here doin' to my brother?"

Jenni was right behind her, looking all around and over her shoulder. "Check his *ass*, girl! Check his *ass!*"

"Ain't nobody do nothin' to that boy!" Raynard pleaded.

Pat leaned over Stevie and went in his pocket, checking and counting his three wrinkled dollars. "Did he try to get yo' money, baby?" she asked.

To Raynard, he was being done worst than any ass whuppin'. There was absolutely nothing he could do to redeem himself.

Later that night, after Jenni left and Raynard saw that a beat down wasn't in the forecast, he sat in the chair with Pat across the living room on the couch.

"I saw your car around there. You might as well get your skinny ass over here and eat me while I watch my shows." She threw her head back in a fit of laughter, and when she brought it down, Raynard was kneeling before her.

He stuck his hands in the waistband of her jogging pants, and while she lifted a bit, he yanked them down, turning his head briefly as the crotch of her panties rubber-banded out of her folds where they were trapped. He licked and lapped everything from her bellybutton to her bung hole until her cum completely lathered his full beard.

Raynard got up washed his face, then headed for the door to find the nearest bridge to leap from.

"Hey, boy..." Pat said, handing him a fifty dollar bill. "You put in work that time!"

Raynard couldn't stop cheesing. "You need anything from the store?"

* * *

Raynard held Pat gently in his arms, setting her down on the mattress. As he undressed, he marveled at Pat's beauty as she lay there in her red summer dress and red heels. Her hair was coifed to perfection and there was a diamond at the end of her sparkly necklace.

He had no idea how sweet things could be in life. He'd finally found a way to have it all—minus the drugs. Raynard would sometimes sing songs when he was happy; songs that wouldn't be written or sang for years. Pat began taking note of that fact. After hearing the songs—even the ones he didn't like—being played constantly over the radio, he knew them all word for word. Since Raynard already knew what would happen for the next fifteen years, he started writing songs that he and Pat would sell to different r&b singers.

The two were on the way back from New York where they signed a deal with a major artist for a few million.

"Let's stop and chill in the Poconos for a few days. Ain't like we gotta rush back to go to work." He knew Pat would be down. She seemed to be down with pretty much whatever he said. She had tons of faith in him. She even listened when he told her to keep her diet healthy. She followed him everywhere, including the gym. He could tell she was amazed at the way he kept coming up with hit songs and different inventions. He never told her his secret, but kept her plenty happy. He'd finally found a way to be happy himself.

Raynard got on the bed between Pat's legs, reaching under her dress. The two smiled as their eyes met when he felt for her panties and found that there weren't any. He lifted the dress, pausing a second to take in her gorgeous legs. He licked and sucked her inner thigh until she began rubbing the back of his head. He used his mouth to launch an attack on her vulva; kissing and sucking the lips, until, he decided to fire his primary weapon—the tongue. He flicked his way back and forth across her entrance. He found the delicate groove between the inner and outer lips, taking his tongue sideways up it until he reached her clitoris. There, he spelled their names until she squealed with pleasure.

Pat lifted his head and looked into his eyes. "Baby, please promise me you won't leave me again like you do sometimes."

"I promise," he told her. His mind flashed back to after he copped his blows.

He went into the bedroom and shook the powder from one of the blows out onto the cd cover. He sat staring at the small pile, rolling and lumping his jaw muscles as he thought. Raynard cringed as he realized he was the new puppy nuts. He knew where he wanted to be; he knew what it took to get there. As he dropped two more blows worth of diesel onto the cd cover, he decided to stay.

END

Other books by E. Scrill :

Drug Lords

Children of the Night

To place an order, visit us on the web: www.streetinkbooks.com